Tay-Tay

I saw this book and thought of you. Hope enjoy it, as much as I enjoyed laughing at it.

purity

JACKSON PEARCE

Little, Brown and Company
New York Boston

Copyright © 2012 by Jackson Pearce

Little, Brown and Company

Hachette Book Group
237 Park Avenue, New York, NY 10017
Visit our website at www.lb-teens.com

Little, Brown and Company is a division of Hachette Book Group, Inc.
The Little, Brown name and logo are trademarks of Hachette Book Group, Inc.

The publisher is not responsible for websites (or their content) that are not owned by the publisher.

First Edition: April 2012

Library of Congress Cataloging-in-Publication Data

Pearce, Jackson.
    Purity / by Jackson Pearce.—1st ed.
        p. cm.
    Summary: Sixteen-year-old Shelby finds it difficult to balance her mother's dying request to live a life without restraint with her father's plans for his "little princess," which include attending a traditional father-daughter dance that culminates with a ceremonial vow to live "whole, pure lives."
    ISBN 978-0-316-18246-1
    I. Title.
    PZ7.P31482Pu 2012
    [Fic]—dc23

2011027351

10 9 8 7 6 5 4 3 2

RRD-C

Printed in the United States of America

For Mom and Dad

5 years, 352 days before

When I said it, I didn't mean it. I just wanted to go home after another long day in the ICU. But then, I didn't know it was really the end this time.

"Promise me something," my mom said, her voice cracking, a whisper over the hum of machines that latched onto her body. Sometimes I thought those cords and tubes and electrodes were the only things holding her here. Without them, she'd slip away like a balloon string sliding from a child's fingers.

I nodded, ignoring the pain in my wrist from grasping her hand over the railing. It was an old pain, a dull ache I'd gotten used to, just like the way my spine begged to be stretched and my lungs longed for air without the scent of rubbing alcohol and gauze. Waiting in a hospital for a few months will do that to a body, I guess—even the body of a ten-year-old.

Mom's fingers were frail, and her skin seemed too big for the bones underneath. She smiled, pulling at the tape holding a tube into her nose. "Promise me, Shelby, that you'll do three things. For always, from here on out." She spoke like this a lot — like it was the end. It used to scare me, but after so many months I'd sort of gotten used to it.

I kissed her palm the way she used to kiss mine when she put me to bed. Back when I let her read me picture books long after I'd lost interest in them just because I could tell how happy it made her.

"Sure," I said, ignoring my dad at the door. He was giving me the "five minutes" hand gesture in between intense whispers to a nurse.

My mom rubbed my palm with her thumb, then continued. "Three things. Listen to your father, Shel. Love and listen to him." She paused, and remnants of a laugh laced her voice when she spoke again. "Poor thing doesn't know what to do with a girl." She reached up and ran a hand through the tips of my overgrown hair.

"Okay, Mom," I sighed. "But if this is about that thing with the makeup, it's not fair. Dad says I can't wear *any*."

My mother shook her head. "I know. It's not about that. Listen — second thing: Love as much as possible."

I raised an eyebrow. My mom had always been a dreamer, but this was a little intense even for her.

"Okay, I will," I said as my dad held up two fingers. "I have to go soon —"

"And last," she cut me off, her lips trembling a little, like she'd cry if she had the energy, "live without restraint. Do you understand what I mean?"

Not really — I had no clue what she was talking about. One minute left. I stood, leaning over to hug her — she wasn't

2

much bigger than me, and my arms felt strong around her body. "Sure."

"I mean it, Shelby. Promise me," she said as she hugged me back, her voice growing louder than it'd been all summer, desperation on every syllable.

"Okay, Mom," I said, sincere. "I promise. All three things. I'll do them."

My mom relaxed. The nurse walked in to inject her IV with a clear fluid. I unwound my arms from Mom's body and waved good-bye as my dad took my place by her bed to bid his own farewell. Two tiny tears dripped down Mom's cheeks; the nurse wiped them away without hesitation.

When I said it, I didn't mean it. I didn't know it was *really* the end. And now ... how could I possibly break a promise made to a dying woman?

35 days before

This thing didn't seem *nearly* as high when I looked at it from the ground.

I cringe and sidestep the rusty rails, balancing carefully on the graying wooden planks. The early summer sun glares at me, reflecting up from the lake water. I sink to my knees and scoot toward the edge.

"You can do it, Shelby!" my friend Ruby calls from below, sprawled on the hood of Lucinda, Jonas's beat-up hatchback. Ruby gives me a thumbs-up and nods emphatically.

"Are you okay?" calls another voice, tinged with worry and concern. Jonas shields his eyes from the sun and tries to look up at me. "You can come down. We can do it another day."

"This is the fourth time we've been out here!" I shout. "I just have to . . . do it." I dare to gaze at the water below.

Promise Three: Live without restraint. Hurling oneself off an abandoned railroad trestle into a lake seems stupid more than it does unrestrained, now that I think about it. I know the water is deep enough for the jump—I've swum in it a hundred times and watched a half dozen other Ridgebrook students take the plunge. But knowing doesn't make it any less terrifying.

"Our bodies are our gardens, our wills our gardeners," Jonas calls.

"What?" I snap back.

"Othello," Jonas says. He's read everything Shakespeare ever wrote and memorized half of it. Usually his tendency to throw out quotes isn't irritating, but when I'm trembling on the edge of a trestle, it's hard to appreciate dead playwrights.

"It means your will can make your body jump," Jonas explains.

"Not hardly," I reply. My body demands I stay put, and is astoundingly persuasive.

Jonas shakes his head. "Hang on, I'm coming up."

Hanging on is definitely something I'm willing to do. I sit back on the wooden planks and watch Jonas struggle to climb the steep bank that leads up to the railroad tracks. The tracks are long abandoned but sturdy, despite the mountain of kudzu overtaking one side.

"Wait, I want to come!" Ruby shouts, jumping off the car. She nimbly scales the incline, overtaking Jonas, who gets caught in a patch of Carolina jasmine. Ruby giggles as she helps free him, and finally the two maneuver toward me. Jonas huffs as they do so—puberty gave him great hair and skin but took away the wiry athlete's body he used to have. I think it's a fair trade, personally—all puberty gave me was what the tactless might call childbearing hips.

"I'm telling you, Shelby, it's not as bad as you think,"

Ruby says, plopping down as if we were only a few feet off the ground. I glance down at the rows of crisscrossed timber that hold the railway — and us — up; they look like a pile of pickup sticks. What if I jump and hit one of those?

Jonas uses my shoulders for balance as he tiptoes around me, staying much farther from the edge. "If you're going to do it, you should hurry. Your dad said to be back by four," he reminds me.

"I know," I sigh, fiddling with the edge of my shorts. *Promise One: Love and listen to my father.* It's made me embarrassingly obedient at times — I've never missed a "be back by" curfew. It's also taught me the value of the "If he doesn't specifically say I *can't* do it, I *can* do it" philosophy.

I gaze across the landscape — mostly trees, bright summery green, but I can make out cars on the bridge across the lake.

Jonas sighs. "Look, the trestle isn't going anywhere. We'll come back sometime this summer —"

"Hey, give her a chance," Ruby cuts in, leaning so far out over the trestle that Jonas gasps. Ruby laughs and swings her multitoned legs off the side — Ruby has that disease that makes your skin lose pigment, but you'd never really know it was a *disease* with her. Her skin is toffee-colored but dappled with patches of ivory. Up here against the blue sky, it looks like a few puffy clouds have taken refuge on her body.

"Would it help if I jumped with you?" Ruby asks.

"You're not wearing a bathing suit."

Ruby shrugs. "Still, would it help?"

I pause. At least this way, I won't be plummeting to the ground alone. I nod and Ruby leaps to her feet.

"Great," Jonas mutters. He tugs his shirt off, tossing it to the ground.

"You're gonna do it, too?" I ask, a grin spreading across my face.

"I can't be the only one not to," Jonas says. He rises, then offers me a hand up. Ruby pulls her tank top off, revealing a sparkly pink bra underneath. Jonas rolls his eyes, but even he laughs a little. I hike up the straps of my bathing suit top and look out over the skyline.

"Okay, try to make your body straight like an arrow," Ruby instructs. "Otherwise it hurts like hell."

"Fantastic," Jonas says.

"Ready?" Ruby asks. Jonas wraps his fingers around mine; I reach down and grab Ruby's as well.

"One," I say. *This is it, Mom. This is for you.*

"Two."

Promise Three.

"Three."

I'm not sure who jumps first, but the next thing I know, the three of us sail through the air, blue sky sliding into green trees toward the lake. *This* is life without restraint; *this* is what Mom wanted for me. We release our hands. I'm scared for an instant, then somehow free.

We hit the water. It jets up my nose as I plummet toward the lake's bottom. I kick off the squishy silt and begin to paddle toward the surface. When I emerge, Jonas and Ruby are already laughing and splashing. I squint up at the trestle and grin.

We swim for a few minutes before heading back to the shore. Jonas opens Lucinda's hatchback and tosses us all old Mickey Mouse towels. I wrap mine around myself while they retrieve their shirts. Then we climb into the car.

Lucinda is decked out with zebra-print seat covers and a skull in place of the gearshift knob. She's not exactly a luxury vehicle, but there's something about her that tells you "Trust me—I've made it this far, haven't I?" Which is why we don't worry when there's a loud bang and the check-engine light starts flashing as we rumble along the gravel road.

We arrive at a stop sign, the intersection of the trestle's tiny road and the main highway. I'm too anxious to wait any longer.

"Where's my list?" I ask Jonas.

He reaches across my lap and into the glove compartment and retrieves his wallet. He removes a folded-up, floppy paper from the billfold—*Life List* is penciled across the top in bubbly handwriting.

"You have a pen?" he asks, spreading the ancient piece of paper across the steering wheel.

"You think I'd forget a pen on a cross-off day?" I say, grabbing one from the bottom of my purse. Jonas takes the pen, then runs his finger down the paper until he finds the item he's looking for. He carefully crosses it out, then hands the list over and eases Lucinda forward.

Life List item one hundred and six: *Jump off the Lake Jocassee trestle like Mom did in high school*. It was added to the list soon after she died—judging by Jonas's handwriting, I'd say fifth or sixth grade. It's right before *Put flowers on every grave in a cemetery* (haven't done it yet) and *Learn all eighty-eight constellations* (accomplished late last year). Jonas loves making lists, and he was the one who'd thought of a Life List to help me keep Promise Three. He's always been its official keeper since the day he began it in the funeral home while we waited for her service to begin.

When someone you love dies, it feels like the ground is crumbling away, falling into oblivion. The only thing you can do is grab onto all the things closest to you and hold on tight. I grabbed onto the Promises, to Jonas, to God.

The first two were there. The last one I could never find.

"Wait, while you have the list out," Ruby says from the backseat as she runs her fingers through her wet hair, "I saw this show about a rocket thing that makes you weightless for, like, thirty seconds. So it's like being in space, only without having to actually go to school and become an astronaut and all that. How badass is that? How many people do you know who get to be weightless?"

I nod. "That's a good one. Add it," I say, handing the paper back to Jonas. Ruby usually comes up with the best list suggestions—she started being homeschooled in ninth grade and spends most of her "study" time watching the Discovery Channel.

"I'll just write down 'be weightless' and put the whole

rocket thing on the digital copy." He scribbles in a vacant patch of the paper when we get to a red light. "I need to laminate this or something, or start a new one."

"No way," I argue. "That one's special. It's got...character."

"It's got chocolate syrup stains on it," Jonas reminds me, making a face. We both know what I mean, though—it's been six years and over four hundred items, one hundred three of which are now crossed out. You don't just start fresh when something has that sort of history, even if there are a few stains.

I twist my hair up in a bun and pull on a shirt over my bathing suit as we head to Flying Biscuit, the restaurant where Ruby works. It's the sort of place with tacky tablecloths and a mostly tattooed staff where every menu item has a clever name. I liked it even before Ruby worked here. It's, like, this little mecca of weird in the middle of a pretty-straitlaced town.

Jonas and I sit down in our usual booth, and Ruby, even though she isn't working, ducks into the kitchen to get us drinks.

"What's the next list item?" Jonas says, spinning his silverware on the table.

I shrug. "I want to get three or four done this summer, though."

He looks up at me and raises his eyebrows. "That's ambitious."

"You don't think I can do it?"

"I think you can do it. I'm just wondering what I'll end up doing because of it. I'm still not on board with the sky-diving one," he says, but he's grinning. Ruby returns with drinks — she's filled her Coke with maraschino cherries and grenadine.

"Why's it so crowded here?" Jonas asks, glancing around — the place is never exactly packed, but more tables than normal are filled.

"Sunday," Ruby says with a shrug. "Lunch church crowd."

"Ah, of course," Jonas says, nodding. He's half Jewish, half atheist — I have no idea how that works, exactly, but it seems to. Ruby stopped going to church ages ago, and I finally bowed out a few years back, when I realized I wasn't getting anything but nauseated listening to a pastor talk about God's plan. It's not exactly heartwarming to hear that the guy you're supposed to be worshipping planned all along for your mom to die.

I look around at the families who had likely come from church — adorable family units with two parents and a few kids, all with hair ribbons and tights. I wonder whether they'd break as easily as our family did if you removed the mother from the picture.

"Shelby?" Ruby says.

"Mm?"

"You're staring at that kid. It's freaky. Almost as freaky as that tie he's wearing. What kind of parent loops a noose around their kid's neck and calls it fashionable?" Ruby says disdainfully.

"That's why Jonas doesn't wear ties," I say, turning back to them. "He's afraid he'll accidentally hang himself."

"That's so not true," Jonas argues. "I'm not afraid *I'll* hang myself. I'm afraid it'll get caught in a door or a motor or a car wheel."

I snicker and Ruby raises her eyebrows.

"What?" Jonas asks, his voice rising. "It happens! It happened to Isadora Duncan!"

"Who?" I ask.

"She was this famous dancer in the twenties. She was wearing a big, long scarf, and it got caught in her car tires. And her neck broke. I don't want my obituary to read 'death by tie,' thanks. Don't laugh at me, Ruby," Jonas says.

"Oh, no, I'm not laughing at you for the tie thing anymore. Now I'm laughing at you for knowing about twenties dance stars."

"It's history!"

"It's precious."

"Shelby?" Jonas asks, waiting for me to choose a side.

"I..." I grin, looking from one to the other. "I have to side with Jonas on this one. It's history. Important, safety-themed history."

"Ha," Jonas says, tilting his chin at Ruby mockingly.

"Yeah, yeah, she just sides with you because she's known you longer. You have seniority," Ruby says, laughing.

Not much longer, but longer. I didn't meet Ruby until after Mom died, whereas I met Jonas in kindergarten. Sometimes it feels like Jonas knows everything about where I've come from but Ruby knows everything about where I'm going. I suspect, between the two of them, they know me better than I do.

"I can eat four today, I think," Ruby says as a giant plate of biscuits is delivered.

"Five," Jonas says, raising his eyebrows. They look at me.

"Four. Maybe. I suck at this," I answer.

"You've just got to learn to keep chewing even after you've had so many they don't taste good. It's all about commitment," Jonas says, looking at Ruby as if they're about to drag race each other.

"Ready, set, *go*."

*   *   *   *

Ruby won the biscuit contest—she ate six. She almost always wins, but that doesn't stop Jonas from competing. And I was right; as delicious as Flying Biscuit's biscuits are, I just can't force them down after the third one. After we wallowed in overfull agony for a while, we head back to my house. My hair is mostly dry and signs of the lake trip are few and far between, thankfully. It's not that I don't want Dad to know I went to the lake; it's that Dad's knowing what I do occasionally leads to questions, which occasionally lead to statements like "Don't do that again," which I can't brush off because of Promise One: *Love and listen to my father.* Promise One means no disobeying, which means my life is a thousand times easier when I just keep Dad in the dark.

"Who's that?" Ruby asks as we pull up to my house. There's a tan car in the driveway.

"I don't know," I say, shrugging. "Probably a committee person. Come in with me. I don't want to get stuck in the small-talk loop."

"Committee people" are the only people who visit my house. My dad doesn't really have friends, exactly—he has fellow board members. Volunteers. Since Mom died, he's been on just about every panel and committee and board that the community has to offer. He says he does it because all the volunteering that people did after Mom died helped him—and he's right, there's something innately therapeutic about an endless stream of casseroles. But I think he really does it because he wants to be out of the house. The more time he gives to the community, the less time he has to think about the family that broke in his hands.

Jonas parks the car and we walk to the house, crushing the dandelions that occupy more space on our lawn than actual grass. I push the front door open. My dad is sitting at the dining room table, which is covered in thick stacks of pink-and-gold paper. In the chair beside him is a man I vaguely recognize—one of the pastors from a nearby church.

"Shelby!" the pastor says. I just smile because I don't remember his name. "We were wondering when you'd get back. We'd love to get your thoughts on the Princess Ball while we're still in the planning stages. The church is the lead sponsor this year. We're really excited about it."

Ah, the Princess Ball. A father-daughter dance and a

Ridgebrook tradition—well, sort of. It used to be huge, but now only a fraction of the girls at school go, always the summer before senior year. I figured I'd skip it, since attending a ball with Dad seems like a contender for a Top Ten Awkward Moments list. Apparently, Dad's awkward radar isn't as accurate as mine.

"Here," Dad says, handing me a pink-and-gold pamphlet. It clashes with the faded wallpaper in our dining room. On the cover is a young girl looking lovingly up at a graying model of a man, the kind who's on shaving-cream commercials.

"Your dad has offered to coordinate all the events, and the decorating committee is already throwing around ideas," the pastor says, smiling. The way he says the word *events* makes it seem like it could be either a carnival or a beheading. I rub the glossy paper between my fingers for a moment.

"Um...okay..." I answer cautiously—obviously, I'm going to try to get out of going. I don't want to get Dad's hopes up by appearing excited. Ruby and Jonas shift behind me.

Dad opens his mouth, but words don't come as easily as they did for the pastor. He hesitates. "Great. Great. It'll be fun." He pauses for a long time. "Where were you this morning?" *Damn.* He almost never asks where I've been.

"We were just swimming," Jonas says, stepping in quickly. If *he* tells Dad, then if Dad says "Don't do that again," it means it's directed at Jonas, not me. Unless he makes it "Don't do that again, Shelby." Yeah, that's a loophole, but

Jonas and I decided long ago that when it comes to the Promises, loopholes are nothing to shy away from.

"Oh. Fun," Dad says, sounding a bit confused. He turns back to the pastor. "Well, we'll touch base again in a few weeks?"

"Sounds great, Doug. See you then. Bye, Shelby!"

"Bye...um...sir." Jonas says you can never go wrong calling adults "ma'am" or "sir." Ruby says you can never go wrong calling someone "baby." I think, in this case, Jonas is right.

The pastor leaves, so I make a break for my bedroom, Ruby and Jonas behind me. We shut the door. Ruby and I slump onto the bed while Jonas takes my desk chair after delicately tipping a pile of clothes off it.

"Are you going to the Princess Ball?" I ask Ruby.

She laughs and raises her eyebrows at me. "Seriously? Me? One, I don't wear pantyhose, and I'm pretty sure Princess Ball security checks that at the door. And secondly, can you imagine my dad at that thing? I don't think he even owns a suit. I don't think he even owns a button-down shirt, come to think of it."

"Let me see it," Jonas says, reaching out for the pamphlet. I hand it over.

"Who *does* go to it now, anyway?" Ruby asks.

"I think the church's youth group. Some people from school still go, too. I don't really know," I say, pausing. "My mom went."

"Really?" Ruby says.

"Yeah. Somewhere we've got a picture of her at it in a dress with puffy sleeves. It's pretty eighties-tastic."

"You're all supposed to wear white. Or, at least, it's *advised*," Jonas says, pointing to the pamphlet. "Though looks like the puffy sleeves are optional." He folds down one side and continues to read the back. Ruby stretches for my hairbrush and runs it through her hair.

"You make vows at this thing?" Jonas says.

"Vows? No, nothing that serious. I think you're supposed to, like . . . learn to be close or to respect each other or to only fight on Tuesday nights or something. Not really sure how a ball teaches you that, but—"

"No, Shel—you take *vows*. It says so on the back," Jonas says, looking serious.

I rise and go to my desk, sitting on the edge while Jonas holds the pamphlet out for me to see. On the back, right above the logos of all the Princess Ball sponsors—the church's the largest and centered—are three sentences in a swirly font that's hard to read.

After a night of dinner and dancing,
the Princess Ball concludes with a ceremony:
Fathers will vow to be strong, responsible men of integrity
and to play a central role in their daughters' lives.
Daughters will vow to look to their fathers for guidance
and to live whole, pure lives.

Okay, no big deal—looking to your father for guidance, that's pretty similar to Promise One anyway. But living a pure life? What does that mean? I snatch the pamphlet away from Jonas and flip it over, looking for some sort of code or glossary. Nothing.

And it's the complete lack of explanation that makes me realize exactly what *pure* means.

"Sex. That's what they mean, right? I promise Dad I won't have sex," I say flatly.

"Looks like it. I guess if the church is the lead sponsor, they can throw some antisex stuff into the ball."

"So what do I do?" I ask, my voice rising. "I can't *vow* something to Dad. I'll have to keep it or I break Promise One."

"Just talk him out of it soon—tonight, before he can get too excited about it. That's all you can do, unless you...I mean, you could take the vow...." Jonas says.

"I don't want to vow *anything* that has to do with my lady parts," I answer quickly. The idea makes me shiver, which sends Ruby into a giggling fit. I look at the happy father-daughter couple on the cover. Dad and I could never be like that anyhow.

"I wouldn't worry about it. Your dad has never put up much of a fight before," Ruby adds. "And besides, you're not the only daughter who isn't going to be into this thing. Not to mention that half a zillion girls in this town have no purity left to promise." Ruby snickers, shaking her head.

"Very true," Jonas says. Some of the girls at the church

who go to Ridgebrook with Jonas and me have reputations that rival porn stars'. I'm sure a lot of it is just talk, but a few have the hickeys and—rumor has it—the herpes to prove it.

We make fun of the pamphlet for a while, wondering who chose the stock art image of the father and daughter on the front and imagining it's really an ad for something funnier, like laxatives or juniors' push-up bras. I walk them out, then turn to sigh at the table covered with Princess Ball paperwork. This is a problem. I've got to solve it tonight.

The doorbell rings an hour later—pizza-delivery guy, as per usual on a Sunday night. It's a little later than normal, I guess because Dad got caught up in the Princess Ball planning. He seems to be feeling the effects of the slight change in schedule when I join him in the kitchen. Two hours later than normal throws a wrench in his love of total, constant order.

I guess that's the only other way Dad and I are alike— when the world fell into oblivion, *he* grabbed onto something, too: predictability. He's a computer programmer, a job that involves ties and coats and routines of waking up, going to bed, eating the same food, and not daring to have a conversation with me that we haven't rehearsed a thousand times before. Keep things the same so the world can't slip away again.

We fill our plates with pizza, then slide into beaten kitchen chairs. Dad immediately picks up the most recent issue of *Popular Mechanics* while I flip on the tiny, sauce-spattered kitchen television.

I run a fingertip along the floral pattern at my plate's

edge, trying to muster up the courage to break the routine and talk about the Princess Ball. I glance in Dad's direction as he nods in agreement with whatever science-tastic article he's reading. He folds a slice of pizza in half and takes an enormous bite. Table manners are not his specialty. It's a good thing he doesn't date.

Doesn't date anymore, rather. At his sister's request, he tried, three whole times, but it didn't go well. I know not because he told me, but because I can pick up a phone receiver and listen in with ninjalike silence—specifically, when Dad called my spastic aunt Kaycee to tell her how the dates went.

> **Date number one:** Told the woman he thought she looked beautiful because "most women are just way too thin these days, but not you!" I believe this was followed by some sort of incident involving dinner rolls.
> **Date number two:** Admitted to having a teenage daughter only a few moments in. Painful for me to hear, but I'm not stupid. Single men with babies reel in women. Single men with teenagers are lady repellent.
> **Date number three:** Wasn't really his fault, but Dad accidentally ate shellfish. He swelled up so fast that he had to be taken away in an ambulance. It's hard to be romantic when your tongue has swelled to the size of an elephant's trunk.

After the third date, he reported to his sister that, clearly, he was cursed. I doubt he would have continued dating even if things had gone perfectly. As far as my father is concerned, my mom was the only woman for him. He loved her brand of disorder: shoes in the middle of the floor, cookies she snatched from the oven before they were done, oldies music she played so loud the neighbors complained, nighttime fairy tales with endings she changed to make them more interesting for me....

But despite my dad's addiction to order, I have to do something unexpected tonight—speak over dinner. I turn down the TV as soon as the show goes to commercial. Nip it in the bud, before he gets too invested in the idea.

"So, I wanted to talk to you about this Princess Ball thing," I say.

Dad looks up at me, confused. I'm not sure I've ever uttered the phrase "I wanted to talk to you" to him.

"Sure, what about it?" he asks.

"Well, is it...um...required?" I ask.

"Well, it *is* a tradition...oh, and speaking of..." Dad rustles around in the leather briefcase he always carries with him—I privately call it a man-purse. "We each have one of these to fill out." He hands me a packet.

I read the letters splayed across the top:

DAUGHTER QUESTIONNAIRE

"They're personal questions. I don't know what your packet asks.... We're supposed to go over them together closer to the ball...." My dad trails off and the room fills with an awkward silence. "There's no right or wrong answer, though." He says that, but whenever your parents are involved, there's a right and a wrong answer. Especially with my dad.

I inhale and continue. "So...I mean, you're sure about this? Did you see on the back that this year it involves... vows?"

"Oh, the vows—yes, the committee thought it'd be nice to end with a little more ceremony than in years past. All the fathers and daughters recite vows after the last dance."

So it *is* out loud. Which means it's definitely official— Promise One is in effect.

"I mean, it just seems like an awful lot to plan, for one? And this packet...I've got finals....I don't know if I'll be much help." I don't mention the fact that finals will go on for only another three days.

"It is a lot to plan, true! Especially since we only have five weeks—"

"Five weeks?" I snap, causing Dad to jump.

"Of course. It's smack in the middle of summer. Always has been—I thought you knew. And last year's committee really left us hanging. Luckily the church is donating their events room for the actual dance, so that's taken care of, but none of the other events have been set up."

Events? There are events at these things? I try another approach. "Sure, sure. But maybe the planning and...um... *attending*...should be done by someone who actually likes this sort of thing? I didn't even go to homecoming."

"You went that one year," he says.

"That was a winter formal. I only went because Jonas's mom said he had to go, so we went together."

"Oh. Well, this is a different sort of thing," Dad says.

I didn't want it to come to this, but it's time to break out the sure shot. The winning topic. The one discussion guaranteed to gets fathers everywhere to shut down and shut up.

"So, these vows...how do they work?"

"Oh, it's pretty simple. At the end of the night, the fathers and daughters will read vows to each other. You don't have to memorize anything. It's all off a card we'll get."

"Yeah, but...the thing about being 'pure.' What does that mean, exactly?"

My dad's face turns red, and hints of sweat emerge on his brow. He ruffles the edges of his magazine. "Well, um, it means to not do things like drink underage. Or do drugs. Or...have sex." When he says "have sex" his voice sounds stretched out and pained, like plastic wrap pulled tight.

Great. I wasn't planning on starting up a meth habit or anything, but I would like to potentially have a beer in college. Still, promising to wear an invisible chastity belt is the worst of the three. *Come on, Dad, you know this is stupid....*

After a few moments of the most uncomfortable silence I've ever experienced, Dad doesn't give in and say I don't have to attend. I've got to dig deeper.

"So, what if I have questions about all that, then? Should I ask you, then, since...well, if I'm swearing my purity to you?"

"Um, well, there's no need to discuss those things, really,

because you'll know more about them when you're older and ready to get married and those questions need to be answered."

"But what if I'm curious about those things now?" I press. *Come on, Dad, crack.*

He reopens *Popular Mechanics.* "Well, Shelby, that's why I got you that book."

That book. *Your Body, Yourself.* Having never discussed the whole period thing with my mom before she died, I went to the bathroom once and was pretty sure I was hemorrhaging to death. I was eleven. I screamed a lot, cried a lot, and begged my dad to drive me to the hospital. Instead, he drove me to the bookstore and Aunt Kaycee's house.

"Yeah...the book..." I trail off. "I guess I'm just saying that it's okay if you want to skip the ball. That's all."

My dad sighs and looks up from the magazine, practically begging me to end the conversation. "I really want you to do the Princess Ball, Shelby. Your mom did it. Besides, it'll be fun. You'll get to wear a fancy dress."

I consider reminding Dad that I'm not five, so the fancy dress doesn't quite have the same appeal. I consider yelling at him that the very idea of a Princess Ball is ridiculously misogynistic. I consider breaking Promise One and ignoring the fact that he's blatantly said he wants me to go to the ball, ignoring the Promise to love and listen to him.

But instead, I force a tight smile, nod, and rise. My mom went to the Princess Ball; he wants me to go. How can I argue with that? I set my plate down in the sink and grab another

Coke from the fridge, then bolt to my bedroom. *Don't panic. Don't panic. Don't panic yet, at least. Wait till you're in the room....*

I shut the door.

Okay. Panic now.

I slam the Coke can down on my desk and open it, taking a long drink, as if it's something stronger than colored corn syrup.

He said it. I can't just pretend he doesn't want me to do it, because he said it. Which means Promise One is in effect. Which means holy crap, I *have* to take a vow of purity to my dad. And I'll have to keep that vow because of Promise One.

It won't be so bad, an inner voice tries to calm my quickly heightening nerves. *You can wait till you're twenty-one to drink. And plenty of girls get married as virgins.*

Yeah, a dark voice adds. *Those girls get married at twenty-two, not thirty-five. And you don't want to get married at twenty-two. You've got a Life List to get through.*

Fine then, be a thirty-five-year-old virgin. Or break Promise Three by getting married young and not living life without restraint. Young married couples can't just pick up and travel or adventure or explore—they have jobs and obligations and Tupperware parties. Either way, a Promise gets broken.

I feel like I'm being tested—how crucial is it, really, that I keep the Promises? This is different from jumping off trestles or memorizing constellations—this is *big*.

How important are they, Shelby? It sounds like my

mom's voice is asking me. I imagine her in her Princess Ball gown, puffy sleeves and all.

They're important. They're the most important thing to me. *They're all I have left of you, Mom.*

I have to find a loophole. I've got to find a way to keep both Promises, no matter what it costs me.

At school Monday morning, I head straight for Jonas. We hang out in the fine arts hallway, just outside the band room. It's not because either of us has any musical or artistic ability, but because the asshole-to-awesome-person ratio here is way more in favor of the awesome people. Everyone is flipping through books, trying to cram a semester's worth of algebra into thirty minutes. But compared with the Princess Ball, finals seem like a pretty minor issue to me.

Jonas is sitting on the floor beside Anna Clemens, a former band nerd who found it was easier to quit the clarinet than it was to quit the band's social network. She's talking about some horn line hookup to a punk-rock girl named Christine Juste. I grab Jonas's sleeve and tug him up, then to the other side of the hall.

"I have to do it," I say under my breath. "The Princess Ball. Dad said I had to last night."

"Whoa, whoa, did you try talking him out of it?"

"Yep—that's when he issued the kill order. I might have had a mini freak-out."

"Ah," Jonas says, wrinkling his nose and displacing his

glasses. He reaches up to adjust them, running a hand through his hair. "Okay, so you're looking for a loophole?"

"Exactly."

"I'll think on it," Jonas says, then snickers.

"What's so funny?"

"*You* won't think it's funny," he says, but when I fold my arms he grins sheepishly. "I dunno, Shelby. It's just kind of like a sitcom, thinking of you vowing your purity."

"Even the word *purity* freaks me out," I answer in disgust.

"Exactly. It'd make the perfect sitcom plot."

Together, we walk back toward Anna. I swing my book bag over my shoulder and fold to the ground. Anna immediately begins yammering about someone who was drunk at a party. I tune her out, my head filled with potential loophole plans.

A few hours and two potentially bombed finals later, I'm not any closer to a plan than I was last night. I'm just more frustrated. The only thing keeping me from totally snapping is the fact that final-exam days run only till noon, so by twelve thirty I'm chucking my book bag into Lucinda's backseat.

"Hello, Sunshine," Jonas says. "I might as well tell you now — I haven't thought of anything, either. Your mom's Promises and purity don't really go hand in hand. But I did make a list of sitcom plots involving Princess Balls," he finishes, grinning and holding up a piece of paper.

"Great," I say, ignoring the list. "Is Ruby meeting us at the park?"

"Yep. How did your finals go?" he asks, shoving the paper back into his bag.

"I might have drawn my dad fighting a sexy dragon on my desk instead of finishing my tests," I say, and Jonas laughs.

It takes us a half hour to escape the school parking lot, the midday heat beating down on us with way more force than Lucinda's AC can battle. By the time we're tooling down a wooded road, we're both wet with sweat and humidity.

Ridge Park is a few miles behind the school, and it isn't much more than a field, a fountain, and a playground. Ruby waits for us by the fountain, looking melted. She stares down at her camera, adjusting settings and such, but looks up when we park in the deserted gravel lot.

Ruby collects art forms. This month, she's a photographer. A while back, it was sewing; she makes all her own clothes now. When it was painting, she put this crazy mural of purple zebras on her bedroom wall.

"Hurrah! You're here. Okay, Shelby, you stand on the edge of the fountain," Ruby says. "And Jonas, what she's going to do is just fall off. So you need to catch her."

"What?" Jonas asks. "If I miss, it's concrete!"

"Yeah, yeah, don't miss. Shelby, turn this way. I want the sun behind you so it's just a silhouette."

I look at Jonas and shrug, clearly more confident in his ability to catch me than he is. Ruby sets up her tripod and screws the camera onto the top. Jonas and I take the opportunity to practice; I tilt off the fountain's edge and into his arms, elbowing him in the throat. I apologize, and Jonas, coughing, signals for me to give it another try. The spray of the fountain is calming in the sticky summer air, but it's combining with sweat and making my skin slippery.

"So did you work out the whole Princess Ball thing?" Ruby asks as she adjusts the camera lens.

"Not really. All I got was a questionnaire I'm supposed to fill out and a headache." I pitch off the edge again. Jonas almost misses, but I manage to get a leg down to support myself in time. A lone jogger gives us a curious look as he passes on the other side of the grassy field.

"Ruby, I think professional photographers do this sort of thing over a mat or something," Jonas mumbles.

"Yeah, buy me a big giant mat and we'll do that. Anyway, Shelby, so no sex for you? Taking the Princess Ball vow of prudishness?"

"Not yet—I'm looking for a loophole to get out of it. And it's not just sex—apparently being 'pure' means no drinking or drugs, either."

"I assume you already had no plans to end up on one of those drug-rehab shows, but no drinking, either? Ever?" Ruby asks as Jonas catches me again.

"No, just no drinking till I'm twenty-one. I can deal with that, if I have to," I answer as I climb back up onto the fountain.

"Didn't you have a beer at that Flying Biscuit Christmas party we went to last year?" Ruby asks.

"I did," I admit.

"So...doesn't that mean in the drinking category, you have no purity to begin with?" Ruby says, peering down at the camera and adjusting something. She lifts her head; I fall, Jonas catches me.

"I guess," I answer.

"So you're saying she can vow that and it won't count," Jonas says, nodding. "I can't believe I didn't realize that. It's so obvious—it negates the vow."

I pause, thinking about it. They're right. It's a totally valid loophole. I grin and step back up on the fountain.

"All right, that gets me out of the drinking part. Any genius ideas on the sex ban?" I ask.

"Think you could just quietly switch up the wording, so you're only vowing the drug and alcohol part?" Jonas suggests.

"Apparently we have to read off a card. I'm pretty sure Dad would notice if I skipped something."

"What if you just got conveniently sick on ball day?" Ruby says.

"No way," I answer. "I don't fake sick." It's not even an option—watching someone die of a real sickness will make feigning a headache seem like a pretty crappy thing to do. I fall again, and it's silent while I climb back up. I prepare to fall again, start to lean—

"I've got it!" Ruby shouts, so loud I lose my balance— Jonas had snapped his head toward Ruby but looks back just in time to keep me from smashing into the ground. He glowers at Ruby as he helps me stand.

"Sorry, sorry—but I've got it, really. You can treat it just like the drinking ban. You can have sex *before* the ball."

"*What?* That's the stupidest thing I've ever heard," Jonas says as I get back up on the fountain.

"It is not!" Ruby says. "If it works for drinking, it works for sex. And Shelby? You've got to relax on the fall this time," Ruby instructs.

"Sorry," I say. "That seems pretty extreme, Ruby. I mean, I think it's a valid loophole, but..."

"But what?" Ruby asks, snapping another picture. "I thought the Promises were the most important thing. No matter what."

"Fair point," I say.

"Fair point! There's nothing fair about that point," Jonas says. "This is totally different from the drinking thing."

Ruby scoffs as we set up again. "It's not *that* different from any of the things you do to keep the Promises," she says to me. "You didn't really want to jump off that trestle, but you had to. You don't really want to have sex, but maybe you have to do that, too. Move a little more to your right, and don't look so much like you're jumping *at* him."

"Don't move too far to the right—I won't be able to see you because of the sun. But no. No way can you just have random sex like that," Jonas says.

"I never said it had to be random," Ruby says, snapping a few photos as I fall. She pauses as she adjusts the lens. "I mean, you could make a list—hell, Jonas, you love making lists. You should help. Narrow it down, figure out a candidate who isn't going to give you crabs or ask you to pee on him. That sort of thing."

32

"That's disgusting," I say with a laugh, wiping water from the fountain's spray out of my eyes.

"Some dude asked my friend Marjorie to pee on him once. I'm just saying, choose your partner carefully. Hence, *the list*."

"You think you're going to be able to just tell some guy, 'Hey, man, you're at the top of my list of People I Wanna Screw Before a Ball. Would you mind removing your pants?'" Jonas breaks in, holding out his arms for another fall.

"Seriously, Jonas?" I ask. "You really think I won't be able to find a single guy in Ridgebrook willing to have sex with me if I go through with this? Ouch. Way to cut deep." I exhale and fall, trying to relax as per Ruby's order.

"That's not what I meant," Jonas says. "I'm just saying, despite what you see on television, I'd wager that most of the guys sans crabs and sans peeing fetishes aren't the sort to want to, um...*make love* with you just so you can loophole out of a vow."

I laugh so hard Jonas has to put me down right away. The words *make love* have never sounded so awkward. Ruby kneels on the ground to control herself, tears forming in the corners of her eyes, while Jonas crosses his arms.

"Okay...okay..." Ruby says through giggle outbursts as we attempt to contain ourselves. "First off, Jonas, hearing you say 'make love' is just all kinds of special. Secondly, making love is totally out of the question." She turns to me. "Look, Shel, there's getting laid, there's dirty porno sex, there's making love, there's...well, I'm sure there are more.

They're not the same thing. You need to go into this knowing which one you're shooting for. 'Cause if you're trying to make love and you end up getting laid, you'll be disappointed."

I climb back onto the edge of the fountain and pause for a moment, staring up toward the sun. The sky is a bright, nearly cloudless blue, and my vision blurs from water and light. I squeeze my eyes shut this time and fall backward into Jonas's arms.

"If I did this—and I'm not saying I will—which one do you think I should aim for?" I ask as he lets me down. "I mean, making love is out since, well, there's no one I'm in love with."

"I recommend just getting laid. Nice, quick, and commitment-free," Ruby says as Jonas takes my hand to help me back onto the fountain.

I nod—"getting laid" seems the simplest of the three. The least big of a deal. I can handle that. Maybe. As a last resort, anyway, if I can't find another loophole. I pitch backward toward Jonas again, locking my eyes on the sky. A weird, out-of-control-type feeling rushes through my chest, where my body is shouting "no!" It stops when Jonas's arms catch me.

I have to keep the Promises. They're that important— more important than my virginity. I open my eyes as Jonas lets my legs down. Ruby stares at her camera, then begins to unscrew it from her tripod.

"Awesome. I want to see what these look like on my computer before we spend too long out here. But if they suck, you have to come back with me," she says. We trudge back to our cars. Ruby ducks inside and turns the AC on in her hybrid before climbing in.

"Let me know what you decide about the sexing, Shelby," she calls over the roof as Jonas and I open Lucinda's doors. The scent of heat and stale McDonald's wafts out. "Or if you or Boy Genius there can think of something else, because I'd love to know if I overlooked an easier loophole."

"I will," I say, nodding. Ruby grins and slides into her car, then eases out of the parking lot.

Jonas and I sink into our seats, both frantically rolling the hand-crank windows down. I stare out over the park as Jonas backs Lucinda up, finally looking away when the field disappears behind the wall of trees that line the road.

"Look, it's just . . . I know you don't want to take this vow and all, but you can't take Ruby too seriously. Not yet, anyway," he says, slowing as we take a sharp turn. It's one of those roads where it feels like they built around the trees instead of hacking through them. I like that.

"We have to think of something else fast, then," I say. "I can't break Promise One or Three, and right now it looks like the only way around that is Ruby's plan."

"I know," Jonas sighs. "Just give your dad another night or so. See if he stays serious about it."

*   *   *   *

We're back at my house by midafternoon, when the sun is so hot that everyone locks themselves indoors. I hop out of

Lucinda with my book bag, rehearsing telling my dad about how the Princess Ball just isn't my thing. It shouldn't be hard, I tell myself as I turn the front doorknob and Jonas pulls out of the driveway.

Dad is sitting at the dining room table—he's usually at work till at least seven. There are boxes all around him crammed full of Princess Ball stuff; each looks a little like a thief had ransacked them. Typically, this is Dad's element—when he was on the board for a landscaping thing, there was three times this much paperwork and he soaked it up like it was a life force. But right now he looks overwhelmed, surrounded by the giant stacks of paper with a sad look on his face. I feel a twinge of pity, despite the fact that he's the reason I'm stuck with this whole purity problem.

"Hey, Dad," I say, letting my book bag slide off my shoulder.

"Oh, hey, Shelby. You're home from school a little early."

"It's finals week. You're home from work early."

"I'll be taking a few days off work. Ball planning is pretty intense, apparently," he mumbles, pushing a pile of papers across the dining room table. They run into another pile, which pitches forward and slides onto the floor. Dad sighs.

"I'll definitely need help planning it. I'm supposed to pick out events within the next week. Like, for example, one year the Princess Ball included a ballet number. But do most girls know how to dance? You took ballet when you were little, didn't you?"

"Yes." I nod slowly, recalling my days in a frilly pink

tutu. I try not to cringe. "But I don't think I remember enough for any sort of . . . recital thing," I quickly add.

"Okay, so that one's out. . . ." He pulls a piece of paper from the nearest stack, then sets it aside. It's like some sort of relief has washed over him. He picks up another sheet. "What about a letter ceremony? You write a letter about yourself and the vows you're taking, then put it at a cross— oh, wait, this is a carryover from when it was a religious ball. I guess we'd have to put them at something other than a cross—not everyone would want to write a letter to Jesus. . . ."

"Um . . . sure . . ." Letter to Jesus? Wow. I've got a few things I'd like to say to him, sure, but something tells me they aren't Princess Ball–appropriate.

Dad nods and puts the paper in a new stack. He's about to slide another one toward me, but I cut him off.

"I'm not sure I'm really up to planning all this now. I've got to study for a final tomorrow."

"Oh!" he says, then looks sheepish, like he should have known that I'd be busy. "It's just . . . you know, only five weeks out. I was thinking it'd be a breeze. . . ."

I sigh. "Okay, I'll help—but I've got to study. Maybe later?" I say, which is code for "Maybe after I've punched myself in the face fifty times."

I'm already speed-dialing Jonas by the time I reach the top of the stairs.

"Well," I say when he answers, "I don't even need to give it more than tonight. He's a go for Princess Ball badness."

Jonas groans. "And you seriously think exploiting Ruby's loophole is a good idea?"

"I have to, Jonas. We've only got five weeks and I don't have any other ideas."

"I still don't think your mom intended for you to get laid just to keep your Promise," Jonas says.

"Yeah, yeah." Truth is, I'm never going to know what Mom intended with the Promises, just that she wanted me to keep them. "I'm gonna need your help, though," I tell Jonas.

Jonas makes a few stuttered noises, followed by awkward silence.

"Not like that! I'm not asking you to sleep with me!"

"Of course not!" Jonas says, and I can practically feel his face heating up through the phone. He stumbles over words before spitting out, "I was just surprised that you're asking me to help you get some. But anyhow, *no*. I'm not helping."

"Jonas! Come on! I need an insider's advice on which guys at school to go for. You're my best friend. Who else is going to help me?

More silence. I hear Jonas's breathing deepen, like he's trying to keep himself from shouting or hyperventilating. "So what if it doesn't work? What if you don't lose your virginity before the ball?"

"Then ... I don't know. We have to make sure that doesn't happen."

We're silent for a minute. I bite my lip pleadingly, an act that somehow seems to translate over the phone because

Jonas sighs and gives in. "Fine. If you want my help, though, you have to set some rules."

I hear papers rustling and know he's making a list. I can't help but grin.

"Title, title," he hums to himself. All of Jonas's lists have to have titles. "Lose Virginity Now."

"LVN?"

"Better yet, Lo-Vi-N," he says.

"Oh, good one. LOVIN," I agree. "So, rules. What are they?"

"For starters, no one with a reputation for having something contagious. Or something noncontagious. Just no one with a reputation for having anything at all except for normal, uninfected plumbing down below."

"Of course, that's a given," I say, leaning back on my pillows as I hear him scribble that down. "And while we're at it—condoms. Have to use condoms."

"Yes, yes," Jonas mutters, and I can picture him nodding in agreement. "What about a 'no jackasses' rule?"

I muse over the idea. "I don't think that'll work. I've only got five weeks. If we throw out the jackasses at Ridgebrook, we'll be left with, like...the drama club and a few people in marching band."

"What's wrong with that? I've got loads of friends in the marching band. And I'm in the drama club."

I ignore him. "So, with those criteria, anyone in particular come to mind?"

"Off the top of my head?"

"Why not?"

"Because you aren't supposed to pick sexual partners the same way you pick snacks from a vending machine!"

"Will you at least think about it tomorrow at school?"

"Whatever," Jonas says. "Study for your history final."

"I am, I am. Can we go get doughnuts before school, though? I need sugar for brainpower."

"Sure," Jonas says. "I'll pick you up at seven."

"Thanks, Jonas," I say, and I mean it for a thousand different things, which I think he understands.

When we hang up, I stare at my history book for a few moments. I mean to study — really — but that damned Princess Ball questionnaire stares at me. Lurking, there beneath a bunch of papers on my desk. I grab a pink pen and begin to fill in the first page.

1. **Your Name:** Shelby Crewe
2. **Father's Name:** Doug Crewe
3. **Mother's Name:**

Mom told me once that growing up, she'd been determined to never change her name when she got married. When she met Dad, that changed — his last name is Crewe, like the main character in her favorite book, *A Little Princess*. She said it must have been fate, so she changed her name for his. I stare at the blank where her name goes — usually, I would just put a dash or skip the *Mother's Name* part of school forms and stuff, because as awful as it is to dash Mom out of existence, it's way better than how people look at me when I go through the whole "She had breast cancer and died, so no, she doesn't have a daytime phone or e-mail address" explanation. People get this sad look and talk to you in high-pitched voices, then about two minutes later go on to something else. The world keeps spinning, I guess. Even my world.

I wish it wouldn't.

I look down at my hands, clutching the pink pen. Do they look like hers? I can't quite remember. It's like every year, she gets more watery in my head, her features a little less defined without the help of a photograph. I wonder what she would think of all this—I mean, she went to the Princess Ball, she wore a white dress just like I'll have to. But as far as I know, she didn't have to say vows aloud. Would she understand why I can't?

Would she be disappointed in me?

I try to picture myself telling her about it, asking her advice. She'd talk some sense into Dad, I bet. I daydream about lying on my parents' bed, sun streaming in the windows, while she sorts laundry and I ask her what she would do if she were me.

People expect you to miss the big things after someone you love dies. They expect you to think about graduating, falling in love, getting married without your mother there. And I do think about those things. But the things I really miss are smaller, fractions of my life intersected with hers, the moments I didn't bother remembering because they seemed too unimportant—going to the grocery store, coming down the stairs in the morning, watching television, folding laundry. Things that happened a thousand times that will never, ever happen again. It's like a drug that I can't have, yet am hopelessly addicted to; I want those moments all the time. Some days all I do is imagine them, an endless stream of daydreams.

But even in my daydreams, she can't respond. Mom is stuck in time — I can never know what she'd say to a problem I'm having in my life now, especially not this one, because everything would be different if she hadn't died. Daydream Mom just smiles at me, folds a T-shirt, reminds me of the Promises. She doesn't age — she always looks thirty-two in my dreams, the way she looked just before she got sick. What will happen when I turn thirty-four and my mom is younger than I am? When I'm no longer her little girl?

I'll have to grab onto something, someone, just like before, because I know it'll feel like the world is collapsing all over again. I wonder if I'll reach out for God again, only to be completely unable to grab hold.

Maybe. But probably not. I think I'm done reaching out for him.

It's not that I didn't *want* to find God after Mom died. It's not even that I don't believe in him — in fact I believe in him now even more than I did when I was little. When your world is all about your beautiful mom and funny dad and birthdays and pony rides and laughter, the God Sunday school teaches you about seems like another pretty story they just haven't made a Disney movie of yet. But when your mom dies slowly, painfully, while you pray and beg and give just like you're told, your entire world shifts. God is more real than ever—because he's hurt you. And you're forever left wondering why, when you reached out, God didn't *let you* grab on.

I wish he would. It'd be so much easier to blame him that way—so much easier to handle than the thick disappointment in God that I can never really shake. The Promises, however, let me grab on every time. I did everything God ever asked of me and Mom still died—so maybe if I do everything Mom asked...well, *some* good will come of it, surely. I won't be losing my virginity for nothing.

I shake my head and turn back to the questionnaire, eager to push away the gnawing ache in my chest. I've gotten good at casting pain aside. I move on to the next question without writing in Mom's name.

4. Do you have any brothers, close uncles, close male cousins, or other men who play a significant role as a guiding figure in your life?

Well, Jonas, sort of, but I don't know that I'd say he's a man in my life, exactly. Still, he keeps the Life List, he's my best friend. It doesn't get much more "guiding" than that. I write his name in.

5. How much quality time do you spend with your father exclusively on any given day?

Um ... quality time? What is quality time, anyway? Does it count as quality if we just sit together over dinner and try to avoid too much discussion?

I wonder what Dad would say about the LOVIN plan. Not that I'll talk to him about it, of course, but sometimes I daydream about Dad the same way I daydream about Mom — only I think about the dad I would have if he *weren't* torn apart by grief. I pretend he's the kind of dad who goes to the school plays I'd be in if I hadn't quit theater, who helps me make lame science projects, who glares at boys who want to take me to prom and teaches me how to drive on the weekends.

I wonder if he sometimes pretends I'm a different kind of daughter.

I scribble in *one hour* and push the paper aside.

33 days before

The doughnuts don't help me with my history final. By the time I make it out of the two-hour test (which is cruel and unusual punishment, if you ask me), my brain is fried. We have a half hour before final number two of the day; luckily I've never had a big problem with English. I skip reviewing the study packet and sit down beside Jonas in the lunchroom.

"Okay," I say, anxious to get the French Revolution off my mind. "This is our chance. Who is LOVIN plan material?"

"This is still the worst idea I've ever heard," Jonas mumbles, and pretends to read his history study guide.

"Come on," I plead. "I don't want to choose people without your opinion, Jonas. You know them as guys. You've got insight. You've got secret knowledge!"

"The only thing I've got is a serious headache from all this. Come on, can't it wait till after finals?"

"Nope. I've only got five weeks, remember?"

Jonas sighs and sets down his packet, then helps me scan the lunchroom. I'm looking with anticipation; Jonas is looking nauseated.

"Maybe we should take this table by table," I say when I realize that looking at the entire school at once is a little intimidating. Anna Clemens sits down beside Jonas and glances around to see what we're staring at.

"What's going on with you two?" she asks.

I quickly give Jonas a small shake of the head; I don't want anyone else knowing about my LOVIN plan. I may be going through with this, but it doesn't mean I've lost sight of how crazy it is. Jonas sighs and doesn't answer Anna, who turns her questioning gaze to me.

"I was asking Jonas," I begin, realizing just how helpful a girl like Anna could be, "if he thought any guy in school is particularly sexy."

"You asked Jonas that?" Anna asks as Jonas's face turns beet red. "And you were looking, Jonas?"

"Something like that," Jonas says with a scowl.

"He was just helping me out," I say.

Anna shrugs it off and scans the room. "I don't know about sexy, really. Why?"

"I was just trying to figure out how many of them have actually *had* sex, you know?"

"Oh! Well, hell, Shelby, I can tell you that," Anna says, face lighting up. If Anna doesn't know about a hookup, it simply didn't happen. And if that hookup involves the marching band she knows if it happened, the size of all body parts involved, a time frame, and underwear colors.

"Let's see, the entire football table, pretty much, though I don't know if I'd ever call one of them sexy. But then, I'm not into jocks," Anna says with a shrug. "The theater table—Jason and Mike play for the other team, but the rest are straight. I think they've all gotten to the last levels, but only Mark and Nick are on the high-score list. I'd also say most of the horn line has played the game, and the majority of the drum line has gone hot and heavy with a girl or two—usually from the woodwind section. People always figure it's the color guard, but seriously, it's the woodwinds you've got to look out for."

"Good to know," I say, almost sincerely as I analyze the maze of metaphors. Jonas seems to have zoned out, focusing intensely on loose threads at the bottom of his T-shirt.

"Anyway, it's kind of random. Sometimes it's the guys you'd never expect, truth be told," Anna says, looking at Jonas and me with a shrug.

"Right..." I eye the drama table carefully. The king of the drama department is Ben Simmons. He's the sort of guy who is incredibly popular despite not being a jock, but there's nothing quite like playing Romeo to win the heart of every high school girl (and maybe a few young teachers). We were friends in middle school when we were both in drama club; I dropped out when I realized my lack of acting skills would always relegate me to celebrated roles like "Cowboy #6" or "Eager Fan."

"What about Ben Simmons?" I ask. Jonas's head jumps up.

"Oh yeah. He's kind of the man whore of the drama department. I made out with him at a party once, actually. Probably the most popular I'll ever get," Anna says with a sigh.

As soon as the bell rings, I tug Jonas aside. "Put Ben Simmons on the list."

"Are you crazy? I thought you were just entertaining Anna. Ben is an arrogant asshole. You wanted my opinion and—"

"But there's not a rule against jackasses, remember? And besides, he's probably got standards that I can meet without going to the football players. Jonas, come on. . . . He's just an option. Maybe I won't even need him."

Jonas rolls his eyes but nods. "Fine, but he can't be the number-one pick."

"Deal."

I meet up with Jonas at the end of the school day and make him pull out the LOVIN List so I can see Ben's name, which is sitting halfway down the page. Still, having one name makes me feel better, like I'm making progress instead of just accepting my eternal virgin fate.

"Think of anyone else?" Jonas asks as we walk to his car, a defeated sound in his voice.

"Sort of." The name occurred to me in the middle of my English final. He's not the person I'd most like to sleep with, but there are worse choices.

"Who?" Jonas asks.

"What about . . . Daniel?"

"Daniel? Costume Daniel? Ex-boyfriend Daniel?" Jonas asks.

"Sure. I mean, I know he doesn't have any creepy disease or whatever. And besides, we already fooled around a little bit. He's an okay guy."

Jonas studies me for a moment. "Daniel. Really?"

"You sound surprised," I say as we approach the door to the parking lot. People bottleneck here, smashed together like cattle.

"I am. Daniel..." Jonas says as he ducks to avoid getting hit in the face by a girl's giant frizzy hair.

"I've got a better shot with him than Ben, I imagine."

Jonas sighs. "Lord, what fools these mortals be," he quotes as we break out of the cattle herd and emerge in the heat of the day. We squint in the bright sunlight, and the scent of cut grass from the baseball field is heavy in the air.

When we get to Lucinda, Jonas pulls out the LOVIN List and scribbles Daniel's name at the top. "If you're actually going through with this, I guess it's better Daniel than Ben," he mutters.

We'd promised Ruby we would drop by Flying Biscuit after school, and by the time we're there I'm already considering my options for a third guy. Jonas seems sick of hearing about it, so I keep quiet as I race through guys in the marching band. Steven what's-his-name? He's not entirely unattractive. Maybe. But then there's also Alex, a trumpet player who has a reputation....

"So have we come up with a better loophole for the ball? Tell me fast. I've got a table of those Red Hat Society ladies waiting on a messed-up order," Ruby says with a grin. She slides into our booth, braided pigtails swinging back and forth. Her skin looks even more elaborate in the afternoon light, a watercolor of peach tones.

"No, we're still going with your plan, unless you've got a better one," I say. "I have five weeks to find someone—"

"Five weeks? Man. I thought you had more time," Ruby says. "So, who is the lucky winner of your virginity, Shel? Because the new waiter here asked about you. Jeffery? And all I'm saying is, *I* wouldn't throw him out of bed."

"We're making the list," I say, "and at the top is Daniel Caulfield. He's the perfect candidate. We aren't friends anymore, and as far as I know, he's STD-free. No offense to Jeffery—I'd just rather start with people I somewhat know."

"Daniel Caulfield," Ruby says, flipping her order book back and forth as she thinks. "The guy you dated last year, right?"

"Yeah, that's him," Jonas interrupts with a defeated tone. "And that was also the guy she *broke up with* last year."

"That's only relevant if they broke up for a sex-related reason," Ruby says, leaning back to eye the order-up counter. "I mean, if they split because he's all, like, 'Oh, baby, I want to have hot carnal relations with you now in this beanbag chair,' then he's perfect for this—"

"I so don't want to hear this," Jonas cuts her off, then clamps his lips down on his soda straw and slouches, letting his shaggy hair fall in front of his eyes.

I turn to Ruby. "We broke up after only a few weeks because I couldn't compete with his love for cosplay. I refused to miss Jonas's birthday to go to some ginormous costume convention with him. But we *did*, um…fool around a few times. So I don't think sex is too far out of the question."

"How 'around' was this fooling?" Ruby asks. Jonas puts his head down and groans.

"Removal of shirts, reaching under other…um…articles of clothing," I say like I'm explaining a medical condition.

"That's not very 'around'—oh, wait, hold that thought," Ruby cuts in as the cook slides a plate heaped with pancakes under the heat lamps. She hurries over to deliver it to a table of impatient-looking women in elaborate red and purple hats. They look like a bunch of oversize berries.

"I didn't know that," Jonas says, sighing as he sits back up.

"Huh? That Daniel and I—"

"No, I figured *that*. He was always staring at your boobs—no way he wouldn't cop a feel. But I didn't know about why you and Daniel broke up. I thought it was just the cosplay thing. I didn't know the thing about my party."

I prop my feet up on the opposite side of the booth, trying to keep my sundress tucked under my legs. "Well, it was really just convenient timing. The cosplay thing was freaking me out, and your mom told me you'd be getting the car, so…you know. I couldn't miss the unveiling of my primary mode of transportation." I smile, and Jonas laughs, yet shakes his head.

"Fair. But promise me that if he wants you to dress up like Wonder Woman in order to have sex, you'll bail."

"Okay," I say. "He's more of the anime-loving-fuzzy-ear-wearing-girl type anyhow."

"Naturally," he says, grabbing for his glass again as Ruby slinks back over.

"So how and when are you going to get him into bed?" she asks with a candied gleam in her eyes. I blush a little.

"I'm thinking Saturday, just because I can usually get the van on Saturday nights. I'm not sure how, though. I figured I'd just, like...you know, hit on him, and then...I figured I could just—"

"Are you going to tell him you're still a virgin?" Jonas interrupts.

"I don't think so," I say. "What if he gets cold feet?"

"What if he doesn't know and is...rough?" Jonas asks, folding his arms across his chest and raising a bushy eyebrow.

"Good point, Jonas," Ruby says. "Seriously, Shel. If you're hoping he'll tell from your face that he's hurting you, you've got another thing coming."

"Maybe," I say. "I'll just tell him to be careful. I'm not going to explain the whole plan and ball and everything, though. That'd definitely scare him off."

"Good idea. And what about the panties?" Ruby asks.

"Oh, God," Jonas groans.

"The panties?" I ask.

"Yes. I know the kind of panties you wear, Shelby, and if you think those are going to get the deed done, you're putting way too many eggs in the 'He's after what's underneath them' basket."

"Ugh, stop saying 'panties.' That word is totally unacceptable—but besides, I wear cute underwear!" I say. "I'm wearing ones with little flowers—"

"Do they have lace?" Ruby asks, folding her arms so that she looks like Jonas.

"No, but—"

"Exactly. This isn't a guy you've dated for ages who will think you're adorable no matter what. Trust me on this one, Shelby. A matching lace bra and panty set will make you impossible to resist. It's like guys have some sort of irreversible programming when they see them. 'Ah! Lace bra and panties! Allow me to sex you up, please!' " she proclaims in a robot voice.

"That's so not true," Jonas says. "We're not animals—"

"Please, Jonas. Men got brute strength and size. Women got hot bodies and steel-trap minds. It's our leg up in your little male-dominated society."

Ruby has a point. A sexist point, but a point.

By the time I get home, I'm so freaked out about the panty requirements that I'm prepared to run straight to my underwear drawer and try to scavenge for *something* lacy and presentable. I think the best I can do might be some blue ones with happy-face rainbows, honestly. But as soon as I hit the door, Dad is there.

"Hey, Shelby!" he says, using up every ounce of his enthusiasm and conversation ability on the greeting.

"Hey, Dad."

Silence. We stand in the hallway, staring at each other.

"So, I wanted to talk to you about the ball plans again.... It was really helpful last time," he says. He sounds nervous.

"What's up?" I ask.

"Well, um, Madame Garba's School for Dance is sponsoring the ball by giving discounted formal dance lessons."

No. Oh God, no, say it isn't so.

"What do you mean?"

Don't answer that, Dad, please don't answer it.

"Well, as Princess Ball organizers, we should probably take the school up on it. Especially since we don't know how to waltz."

"Dad...um..." What am I supposed to say? That I'd rather walk through a rubbing-alcohol river with feet full of fresh paper cuts?

"I was thinking...just one or two lessons. Nothing big," Dad says.

"When is this?"

"The first would be Sunday evening. Are you busy? If you're busy—"

"No." I sigh. "I'm not busy."

"Oh, good. Good."

We stare at each other a moment longer. I silently plead for an interruption, something to keep me from having to continue discussing ball plans, and to my surprise and delight, my phone beeps with a text from Ruby: *Dont forget to shave your legs!!!!*

I smile a little, and Dad rocks back on his heels. "Well, then, I guess I'll go work on my questionnaire. It's really... big!" he says.

I nod, and we brush past each other, him sprinting for the dining room and me for my bedroom.

I try to push the prospect of dance class with Dad out of my head—ballet class with fourteen other four-year-olds was bad enough, but with Dad? *Focus, Shelby.* You're in control, you have a plan—a plan involving panties and leg shaving that will make the entire ball—waltz lessons and all—just an act. I yank open a dresser drawer. Somehow, picking out underwear calms me, reassures me that I'm the one in charge here.

Lots of white, lots of stripes and flowers and other decidedly unsexy things. Toward the back I find the pair with rainbows; they match a camisole I have. Anna got them for me as a set a few Christmases ago. We aren't close, but all her female friends got camisole sets in snowflake-shaped tins that year—probably spoils of an after-Thanksgiving sale. I don't wear either piece of the set too often. I wonder if the camisole counts as a matching bra. Probably not. I just won't tell Ruby.

I try them on in front of a mirror, trying to look sexy—apparently, the lips-parted, sexy faces those Victoria's Secret models make are an acquired skill, because I just look like I'm about to drool. The AC is on high, and it gives me chill bumps, making me look more like an uncooked turkey than sexy. Whatever. I have to call Daniel. No way around it. I might as well do it while I'm wearing my sex gear.

Daniel's number is still in my cell phone. We didn't have a rough breakup, but we definitely haven't called each other since. I scroll down to his name, inhale, and dial, staring at the little rainbows on my underwear. *This is crazy. This is so crazy.*

Daniel answers on the third ring.

"Hello?" he says, and I can tell by his confused tone that his cell's caller ID has already told him it's me.

"Hey, Daniel!" I say, sounding like my dad a half hour ago.

"Shelby? What's up?"

I could get out of this. I could just ask him for directions somewhere or if he still has my favorite bracelet or something. But the Princess Ball pamphlet is peeking out from underneath my history book, screaming "You'll be a thirty-five-year-old virgin!" and it's very persuasive.

"I um...I dunno. I just wanted to talk, I guess."

"About what?" he asks. I hear a few clicks of the computer mouse in the background.

"I just...we haven't really hung out or anything since we stopped dating, and you know...that sucks. I was thinking maybe we could get together Saturday night and watch a movie or something?"

Daniel pauses. "Sure...I'm busy Saturday, though. What about Sunday?"

"Um..." I sigh. "Can it be later? Like, after eight?" I can't believe I have to schedule a dance class and a sexual experience on the same day.

"Yeah, no problem. Any specific movie? What theater?"

"Oh, not a theater," I say, a little too excitedly. I rein myself in. "I was thinking you could come over here or I could go there...."

"Okay," Daniel says, his voice still framed with doubt, like I'm going to pull some sort of huge practical joke on him at any given moment. When I don't speak, he continues. "Want to meet here Sunday night, then? Maybe eight thirty or something?"

"Sounds good. See you then."

And we hang up. Was that all it took for me to schedule a LOVIN date?

Well, maybe LOVIN date. Who knows if he'll actually *do* it. Who knows if I'll actually be able to do it, for that matter. I sigh and stare at myself in the mirror. I can do this. It's not a big deal. I speed-dial Jonas and flop onto the bed.

"Did you talk to him?" Jonas asks.

"Yep. We're meeting up Sunday night. I was thinking I'd have my dad drop me off on the way home from dance class."

"There are two things incredibly wrong with that sentence—one, your dad driving you to a sexcapade, and two, dance class?"

"I have to learn to waltz. Princess Ball thing," I say. "But anyway—tomorrow night, can you take me to the grocery store? Target? Walmart? Some place like that?"

"Yeah, there's a new video game I want to grab anyway. Why?"

"I'm going to need condoms," I say. "And some new razors. Ruby sent me a text earlier threatening me with death if I didn't shave my legs, and I'm all out."

"Wait, seriously? I have to drive you to get condoms?"

"Either that or I try to buy them at a gas station by the school, and I don't trust the ones that have been hanging behind the cashier for a year and a half."

Jonas sighs. "Fine. After school."

"Thank you, Jonas. Seriously. I owe you so big. Like, huge. Whatever you want."

"Sure," Jonas says, and I know he's rolling his eyes at me. "I have to go."

"To do what?"

"Play video games for four hours so I can forget about your imminent de-virginizing," he says.

I laugh and we hang up, but as soon as the phone is off, my laughter stops.

Jonas said it. It's real. I'm imminently going to be de-virginized.

Well, hopefully.

I lie back in bed and stare at the ceiling. When I was making lists with Jonas and thinking about panties and everything, it was just an idea, nothing more. But now there's a date planned, a time, a person. This isn't the way you're supposed to lose your virginity. Not that I really know how you're *supposed* to do it—marriage bed, one-night stand, backseat of a car—but still. I wish I could ask Mom what to do. Part of me even wishes I could ask Dad what to do—a small part, and a stupid part maybe, yet there it is. I wish someone knew the answers.

But my heart is more attached to the Promises than it is to my virginity. It's not a big deal. I repeat the phrase over and over in my head until I've almost convinced myself. *Don't think about it too hard, Shelby.* Like Ruby said—I'm not trying to make love. I'm just trying to get laid.

I hurriedly look around for something to occupy my mind and grab the questionnaire. What would Dad say if I just refused to finish it? No, no, it'd hurt his feelings. I don't want that, even though this whole thing is his fault. . . . I sigh and grab the pink pen off my nightstand, then turn to the second page.

6. What do you feel you have in common with your father?

This is an easy one. We have nothing in common, except maybe that we loved Mom. I leave the answer space empty, then fold the questionnaire into crooked halves and throw it across the room.

32 days before

The next day—the last day of school—Jonas is late getting to Lucinda in the afternoon. He's the kind of guy who swings by the classrooms of his favorite teachers to wish them a good summer. By the time he makes it outside, I'm puddling in sweat and the parking lot is near empty.

"Sorry," he says as he unlocks Lucinda. "So...am I taking you home?"

"Come on. It won't take long."

"Time is not my concern," Jonas says. "It's taking you to buy condoms for a one-night stand. It's creepy."

I ignore the comment as Lucinda struggles to get her air conditioner going. It's just getting into high gear when we reach the nearest grocery store. I hurry to the pharmacy with Jonas trudging bitterly behind me.

My excitement fades when I see the pharmacist—an old, kindly looking man with half-circle glasses and a soft, pink face. He's ringing up a mother holding a young boy, and before sliding the bag across the counter, he drops two green lollipops into it. The little boy grins, the pharmacist waves, and I'm pretty sure I'm in a real live drugstore commercial.

I take a detour by the cold medicines, a desolate aisle, given the ninety-three-degree temperature outside. I spy on the counter while I pretend to read the potential side effects of NyQuil. The condoms are in a locked case right underneath the pharmacy counter.

"What are you doing?" Jonas asks, glancing from me to the NyQuil and back again.

"They're in a case! Why the hell are they in a case? Let's go somewhere else."

"Oh, no," Jonas answers, crossing his arms. "I'll drive you to get the condoms, but I'm not taking you on a tour of the area's finest condom purveyors. Buy them here. You just have to ask the pharmacist for the key."

My stomach is swirling. "No, no. What if he thinks I'm a whore? What if he says something? Oh, man, he looks like my grandfather. I thought this was just like buying Tylenol or something. I didn't know there'd be a case...." I chew on my nail.

"Well, while you study the effects of NyQuil on nursing mothers, I'm going to buy some ice cream," Jonas says, shaking his head. He moves to step away, but I grab his arm.

"Jonas, buy them for me. I'll pay you and buy your ice cream."

"If you're ready to have sex, you're ready to buy condoms. You're on your own."

"This is so unfair."

"No, unfair is you keeping me from the ice cream section," Jonas says. He tries to hide it, but I see tiny hints of a smile tugging at the corners of his mouth. He doesn't think I'll do it. He thinks I'm going to chicken out.

Not a chance.

"Fine. I'll buy them," I say firmly, straightening my shoulders and flipping my hair back. Cool, confident, no big deal. Just buying some condoms. Just a normal grocery run. That involves condoms. I turn sharply on my heel and stride toward the waiting pharmacist, trying not to see too much of my grandfather in his wrinkled face. I focus on his white coat instead. My stomach twirls.

"How can I help you?" he asks warmly, folding his hands like he's preparing to read me a bedtime story.

"I, um..." I rub my lips together. Jonas snickers behind me.

"Ineedthekeytothecase." There. That wasn't so bad. Cool. Collected.

"I'm sorry?" the pharmacist says, leaning closer and cupping a hand behind his ear.

"The case," I repeat, my jaw tight. "I just need the key." I jab my finger downward, indicating the locked glass case. What do they think these things are? Fine jewelry?

"Oh. Oh!" he answers. His pale blue eyes leave mine to focus on the worn counter. He grabs a green lanyard from the register and slides it toward me.

I duck down, jamming the tiny key into the case and yanking it open. The hinges squeal loudly, alerting everyone as far away as frozen foods that someone is planning on getting laid. There are neat little rows of boxes with bright coloring. My eyes scan over them, mind cluttering with words like *intense* and *heated* and *tropical*—tropical? Is this a display of contraceptives or a line of fruity alcohols?

Footsteps behind me; a new customer blocks out the fluorescent lights and darkens the case. I grab the closest box, nearly crushing it with a death grip, and stand. My eyes flicker to the customer behind me—a young woman, belly bulging with pregnancy. God has a twisted sense of humor.

"All right, then," the pharmacist says, still avoiding my eyes. He takes the now-crumpled box from my hands and swipes it across the register. The computer beeps angrily. "Hmm," he says. "These aren't ringing up." He swipes it again. "Let's see," he says. "Oh! That's right—these are the flavored ones. I have to key it in. How much are they?"

"I—" I pause, certain my hair is moments from igniting because of the heat rising off my face. "They're—"

"Seven ninety-nine," the woman behind me says. Her sweet, angelic tone doesn't keep me from grimacing.

"Right, seven ninety-nine. Here you go, then," the pharmacist says, stuffing the condoms into a paper bag before dropping in two lollipops on top of them. I hand over a crumpled ten-dollar bill and tap my foot, waiting for change. By the time I have the bag tucked under my arm, I'm fairly certain another hour has passed. I wheel around, eyes scouring the pharmacy for Jonas. He's lit up in silent hilarity, grin hidden behind a hand clasped over his mouth.

"Oh, shut up," I snip as we walk toward the door.

28 days before

Sunday eventually rolls around, and before I can offer my virginity to Daniel Caulfield, I must bow at the altar of Madame Garba. Dad and I pull up to the dance studio after a long, silent car ride. We both stare at the door like we're afraid a tutu-wearing monster might be lurking on the other side.

The door flies open, but instead of a fire-breathing monster, a crowd of women with their hair in tight buns floods out, all giggles and loud talking about dinner plans for the evening. With a deep breath, I walk inside.

"Which class?" Behind a wooden desk and in front of a wall covered with posters of ballroom-dance couples, a youngish woman taps a pencil against her lips with a bored glaze in her eyes, then repeats the question.

"Dad? Which class?" I ask.

"Waltz 101? We're from the group doing the Princess Ball?" Dad says. I think he's hoping the class is full or canceled; it's definitely what *I'm* hoping. Unfortunately, the woman nods, takes Dad's twenty-five dollars, then points to a room down the hall.

We weave down the hallway, past signed black-and-white photos of dancers, to a crowd of people—fathers and daughters—waiting outside the last room. The classroom is filled with elementary-school-aged kids prancing around to a Latin beat, way more comfortable with being partnered up than I would've been in fifth grade. The music ends, and the flashy teacher dismisses the class. They applaud politely. As they gather their things and file out into the arms of waiting, proud parents, our class meanders in.

The room smells of lemon cleaner laced with the underlying musty scent that all old buildings seem to possess. Unfortunately, there's not much to *look* at in a dance room, other than yourself reflected nine zillion times in the mirror. Dad and I mostly stare at our feet, until I hear my name from across the room.

"Hi, Shelby!" a sweet voice calls out. I look in its direction and see a blond-haired, blue-eyed Barbie girl. Mona Banks.

"How are you? I haven't seen you at youth group in ages!" she says. Her dad is right behind her; he and my dad shake hands cordially and make small talk.

"Yeah, I'm just…busy, you know?" I say. The tiny cross necklace she's wearing glints proudly. If she had a theme song, it'd be "Jesus Loves Me." Sung in rounds.

"Oh yeah, it's tough to fit things in," she says warmly. "We've been doing a lot with the downtown soup kitchen, and it's been taking so much time." See, this is why it's impossible to hate Mona. She volunteers at soup kitchens. She came to my house after Mom died and helped me clean my room. She probably finds orphaned kittens and bottle-feeds them on a weekly basis. But the fact that she's this excited about God after seeing the soup kitchen, my mom's coffin, and orphaned kittens makes her voice grating and her bouncy hair infuriating. Why doesn't she feel let down, like me? Why doesn't everyone?

Truth is, part of me is jealous of Mona. She believes what her Bible and pastor tell her, and so everything in her world makes sense. There's just the complete, total confidence that God loves her. I wish I knew how she found that confidence, that certainty—how God is always there when she reaches out.

I sigh.

"I heard you and your dad are planning the whole Princess Ball!" she says brightly.

"Something like that. I'm just helping out here and there," I say, finally forcing the corners of my mouth into a smile.

"It sounds so fun. I bet it's just like planning a wedding," she says. "All the flowers and dancing..."

I frown. "You know, it actually is like planning a wedding. How...weird." *Weird* is the softest adjective I can come up with, but it isn't exactly the one I want to use. I cringe when I remember seeing something in Dad's stack of papers about a ring ceremony. Marrying Dad. Awesome.

"Let me know if you need any help," Mona says. "I've been planning my wedding since I was, like, three. I have this idea with orchids...."

I never thought I would be so grateful to hear the words "Ladies and gentlemen, our waltz lesson begins now!"

While Mona goes back to her father, a tiny old woman makes her way to the front of the room. She has a cane, but doesn't seem to really need it for balance, and wears a very tight black shirt that looks surprisingly good on her. She's trailed by a young blond man who looks like he might be an underwear model. He sighs when he checks his watch. The room twitters into silence as the woman clasps her hands at her waist.

"I am Madame Garba," she says, coughing, decades of cigarettes and a German accent in her voice, "and this is Waltz 101. Welcome."

A few students politely applaud; I don't catch on till the clapping is almost over and end up giving out a single, loud clap at the very end. Garba gives me a hard look.

"Moving on. The proper waltz position." Garba grabs the hand of the underwear model and slams it against her waist with a devilish sort of grin. She places her corresponding hand on his shoulder, then grasps his other hand in her leathery fingers. She tilts her head back slightly, and there's a hint of old Hollywood in her—like she might have been a starlet back in the day.

"Watch your arms. See how they stay lifted?" she snaps. The class nods obediently. "Then assume the position!" she says, dropping her partner's hand. She walks over to an old CD player and starts a muffled-sounding song.

My dad turns toward me. We both grimace. And we assume the position.

At the sixth-grade formal, there was a kid named Michael who hadn't figured out the proper use of deodorant and was covered in speckled, diseaselike facial hair. I felt bad for him, so I danced with him—after all, at eleven my hair looked like a cracked-out poodle's, so who was I to judge? But when I say that we "danced," what I really mean is this: I left my arms stiff around Michael's neck, locking my elbows so he couldn't wander any closer; he let his hands sit on my hips with all the tenderness of an assembly-line robot; and we rocked back and forth, out of time with the music. I remember counting down the moments till the song ended and I could dash back to the refreshment table and drink sherbet punch.

But I would give just about *anything* to be dancing with Michael instead of my dad right now.

Here, there's no refreshment table or sherbet punch. Just the slow, painful clicking of the clock and the never-ending piano song. Dad and I stand as far apart as possible, and we lean backward like the other has something horribly contagious, perhaps the bubonic plague.

"Ladies, step back here; gentlemen, forward. And one-two-three, one-two-three, see-how-I-step-two-three. Now, you do it." Garba abandons her partner and begins to clap, the sound so sharp that I worry her tiny wrists are going to snap in half.

No one moves.

"Now you do it!" she repeats. Her tone implies an "or else," and no one wants to see the punishments an ex-starlet can dish out. Everyone fumbles into the steps. Dad and I klutz around, each of us dancing to an entirely different beat. Dad stares over my shoulder while I watch the rest of the class in the mirrors. They look beautiful and happy, and I can picture them waltzing around in formal wear. I look like I don't have knees. I grimace as I stomp on Dad's foot, and we accidentally make eye contact for a fifth of a second.

"Yes, yes!" Garba cries. "*Now* you are dancing!"

I disagree. What I'm seeing in the mirror more closely resembles helping a drunk friend stand than it does dancing. I watch the other girls, trying to take notes on what they're doing that I'm not. I recognize their faces from school and my church youth group days, but now they look less like my peers and more like models for the Princess Ball pamphlet. They so seamlessly slid into the part of devoted daughter. Do they really care about the ball and the vow? Are they even virgins to begin with?

It doesn't matter. Liars or not, they're the girls the church, their fathers, the Princess Ball, and my father want to see, and I'll never be them, no matter what dance I learn or what vow I take. I'll always be the one without a mother, the one who questions God, the one who takes vows seriously. I look down at my father's and my feet shuffling clumsily over the floor, a more welcome sight than fifteen pamphlet photos.

"No, the other foot," Dad whispers.

"How do you know?" I ask.

Dad avoids my eyes as he answers. "Your mom made me take dance lessons before our wedding. She wanted to start off dancing the waltz, then break out into 'Thriller.'"

"I didn't know you did that!" I say, louder than I intended and unable to hide a grin. My voice draws a stern look from the instructor. Luckily, another couple backs into her and she's distracted again.

"We didn't," he says. "I finally got the waltz okay, but 'Thriller' was a little out of my reach."

"Yeah, no offense, Dad, but you don't seem the type to rock out to Michael Jackson."

"I know. We waltzed, though, briefly. That's the key: only stay on the dance floor long enough to make everyone think you know the steps, then get out of there before you lose the tempo."

"Don't we have to do the whole song at the ball?" I ask.

"Yes—oh, sorry," he says as he steps on my foot. "But I figure one of us can fake an injury before too long."

I laugh—too loud. The couple next to us look over, but in doing so they tangle their legs together and almost fall. Dad snickers under his breath and I realize I can't remember the last time we laughed together.

Class goes by faster than I expected—a *little* bit. I suppose time flies when you're trying to not fall over or get stepped on, and to keep your arms up. Madame Garba bows as we politely applaud; I race for the door before Mona can stop me to talk.

Outside, it's already dusk. Cicadas have started shouting

from the trees, and the blistering heat from the day has faded to calm, lukewarm air.

"That was, um..." Dad says as he starts the car. "That was interesting."

"To say the least," I say. "Remember, you're dropping me off at Daniel's."

"Oh, yeah. Right." Dad pauses. "Are you still dating him?"

"No," I say, a little surprised—I didn't know Dad realized we were ever dating. "We're just hanging out."

"Good, good," Dad says. "You know, his mom was on the historical committee with me. She was nice. Nice people..." He nods, playing with the keys in the ignition for a moment. I fiddle with the lock on the door.

"So...are you dating anyone?" Dad asks. His voice cracks, like it's confused about how to say those words.

I cough. "No. Not now," I say, still surprised. I've always thought Dad overlooked the fact that I'd aged—like when he saw me, he had that feeling you get when someone you haven't seen in years shows up. You're confused that they look so different even though you know time has passed, so it makes sense that they've changed. Since I was ten, that's how Dad has treated me—like he's confused that I could have changed so much and can't make sense of the current me versus the ten-year-old me he remembers. Sure, he knows I'm sixteen; I just didn't realize he *really* knew—knew enough to ask me about dating.

"What about Jonas?" he asks after a strange, stilted moment passes. He coasts through a stop sign.

I laugh. "Jonas is my best friend."

"Oh. Sorry, I didn't mean..." Dad explains fast, like he's afraid I'm mad.

"It's fine," I say quickly.

The car falls silent. I refuse to think about my destination or the sea of awkwardness Dad and I just sailed through. Instead, I think about the class and, eventually, about "Thriller." About my mom wanting to dance to Michael Jackson at her wedding. Mom loved to dance. When she was in remission for a little while, I came downstairs to find her dancing around the living room, spinning, crashing into the couch. I thought she'd lost her mind, but when I tried to stop her, she just pulled me into the dance.

"I've been too sick to dance for two years," she yelled across the bad nineties music. "Come on, Shelby. I've got a lot of dancing to make up."

And so I gave in and we crashed around the living room, singing the choruses when we knew them. Dad showed up and laughed and wrapped his arms around Mom when a slow song came on, and they slow-danced together. I wonder if they were thinking about their wedding, the "Thriller" dance.

"Thriller" at your wedding. That's living without restraint, I think, smiling. Most of my memories of Mom have to do with her being sick or the tiny, fluttering moments between being sick. Sometimes I feel like I don't even know who she was before the cancer got a hold of her—but "Thriller," that's something, a hint to who she was beforehand. I wonder what else Mom did without restraint that I don't know about. Dozens of things? Nothing else at all? Did she make me promise because she lived her entire precancer life without restraint and wanted the same for me, or because she wished she'd done it more often? Would *she* have made a vow of purity? I wish I could ask her—

"Shelby?" Dad says.

We're here.

I don't know how we got here so quickly. I freeze.

"Huh? Oh, sorry. I...spaced out," I say. I grab the door handle and force myself out of the car. No turning back. Promise One and Promise Three.

"I guess I'll see you later tonight?" Dad asks. "Daniel can drive you home, right?"

"Right," I answer quickly. I shut the door and step from the curb onto Daniel's lawn. The grass is wet from the heat of the day. I trudge through it as I hear Dad's car pull away behind me. I have to do this. I reach forward and ring the doorbell.

It doesn't take Daniel long to answer. He swings the door open, wearing an old T-shirt and jeans.

He looks at me, like he's evaluating something. "Hey," he finally says, leaning against the door frame.

"Hey."

We stare at each other for a moment before Daniel steps aside and lets me in.

Daniel can afford to do the whole costume-making thing because his mom is heir to some sort of pharmaceuticals fortune. I don't think she actually has a job, yet she still goes to charity galas and owns a yacht and all sorts of stuff. So naturally, Daniel's bedroom is their house's "second master bedroom." It's not only huge, but it also has a wall of video games with a built-in cabinet for a zillion different consoles. The "reading area" has been converted into some sort of costume-making office. The walls are lined with pictures of him and his friends wearing Daniel's various creations. He's pretty brilliant at it. No one else could make the school's mythology club actually look like a horde of Spartan warriors.

"What movie did you bring?"

I hold up a DVD of this eighties movie full of puppets and costumes and weird songs. A strange wanna-have-sex movie, but I thought all the fancy outfits would thrill Daniel. My evil plan has obviously worked, because his face lights up.

"I have the special edition of that! Awesome," Daniel says, taking it from my hands. He walks over to the gross display of electronics and puts it in the player. I sit on the futon beneath his lofted bed, painfully aware that my rainbow camisole straps are slipping off my shoulders.

Daniel fiddles around, pressing various buttons until the movie cues up with surround sound. I cringe at the THX theme that makes my teeth vibrate, it's so loud. He finds the correct remote and joins me on the futon—on the opposite end. I give him a nervous smile, which he immediately returns.

This movie is questionable at best. As is my ability to get this guy to sleep with me, especially if I don't make a move soon. I draw my feet up on the couch and move so I'm leaning against the arm and my toes brush against him. He meets my eyes quickly and, in classic teenage-guy oblivion, goes back to watching the movie.

Ten more minutes pass. I lean forward. Brush my hair back. Laugh at jokes that I really don't think are funny.

Daniel stares at the television, and I can tell he's analyzing glues and costume-sewing techniques and appliqué patterns. I nudge him with my feet to distract him; he looks over at me, eyebrow raised.

"Something wrong?"

"Um…" *Think fast, Shelby, think fast.* "Could I have some water?"

"Oh, yeah. Hang on." Daniel pauses the movie. I grab my cell phone and dial Ruby as soon as he's out the door.

"I'm at Daniel's," I whisper.

"Huh? Oh!" Ruby says, giggling. "How's it going, Aphrodite?"

"Awful, we're just watching a DVD."

"Try lying down."

"What?"

"Well, you're on a floor or the couch or something, right?"

"Yeah, a futon."

"Try lying down on him. Like, pretend to be tired. Come on, Shelby, you've got some natural seduction techniques in there somewhere."

When I hear Daniel's footsteps, I hang up on Ruby and silence my cell phone. I inhale quickly and lie down, taking up the entire futon and lifting my arms over my head so a line of skin is showing between my shirt and jeans. I always see girls doing it in movies. There's got to be at least *some* truth to the trick.

"Here you go," Daniel says. I catch his eyes darting down to my waist as I raise a hand to take a sip of the water I didn't really want. I don't make a move to let him back on the couch. Daniel analyzes my position for a moment, then, without so much as a shrug, sits on the floor, leaning his back against the futon. He grabs the remote and hits play.

Damn.

Daniel's head is right about where my neck is. I sigh.

"So...any conventions lately?" I ask.

"Huh? Ah, no, not really. I went to a big one in Atlanta a while back, but that's pretty much it. I'm taking the stage-craft class next semester, though."

"Oh, finally fit it into your schedule?"

"Yeah. It'll be fun," he says without looking back at me.

"Sounds like it..." *Now take my clothes off, Daniel.*

I inhale and let my fingertips slide forward toward the nape of his neck and stiffly touch the tips of his hair. Daniel tenses for a moment, then leans backward slightly. He turns his head toward me.

"Wait...what are you doing?"

"I, um..." This is the death trap I was afraid of. If I say, "I just need to have sex with you once, that's it," then he'll likely say no. If I pretend that I'm interested in getting back together, then I'm a horrible human being.

76

"Nothing," I say quickly. "I just . . . there are some things about our relationship that I miss." *Ooh, good one. Nice and vague.*

"Okay . . ." Daniel says slowly, but even as he does, his head sinks farther back, until my fingers are fully entwined in his hair. Truthfully, it feels kind of gross. He should probably wash it more often.

Shut up, I tell my inner voice. You're not after him for the hair. You just need to have sex with him. It'll take, like, a minute, probably.

I lean over and tug on his arms, urging him to join me on the futon. In a tangle of arms and legs involving a lot of "Oh, sorry" and "Hang on, let me move my arm/leg/hip/foot," he does so, and a sweet five minutes later we're lying side by side on the futon. The musical number ends in the background.

"So, was this the only real reason you came over? Because you missed . . . um . . . me?"

I pause. "Something like that. Well . . ." Maybe honesty will work? Or something close to honesty, I mean. "I haven't dated anyone since you, and I was just thinking maybe we could . . . do this for a while . . ." I let a hand run up his thin chest as I say it, and he gets chill bumps.

"Right," he says, breathing heavily. His breath smells like Cheetos, but I kiss him.

It's just like I remember — not a bad kiss, but not a great one, either. He could put a little more force behind his lips, I think, and I wish he'd shaved before I came over; the speckling of facial hair scratches the skin around my mouth.

Whatever—I pull him closer to me and don't protest when he puts a hand on my lower back, underneath my shirt. We kiss for a while longer, and finally I decide I'm going to have to take some initiative here. I sit up and pull off my shirt, leaving only the camisole and boring, nonlace bra underneath. He doesn't seem wowed. Damn the girls who wear these thin little shirts as real clothing, desensitizing the male population! I inhale and pull the camisole off.

Daniel has seen my bra before, even had his hands under it, but we never got so far as actually removing it. To be honest, the prospect of it is a little frightening. I bite my lip and try to quell my nerves, then lie back down to kiss him again. Finally, the Cheetos smell has dissipated. Daniel moves to pull his shirt off, displaying a level of pale skin that rivals any white powder makeup he has in his collection.

Stop being a bitch, Shelby. You dated him. You put him at the top of the list. I press my boobs against his chest. He shudders, but I take it as a good sign and kiss him again. Halfway there, I tell myself.

"Whoa," he exhales, grinning. "It's been a while...."

"It has," I say. Should I take off more clothing? Probably. I lean forward and kiss him again, and while I do, I unbutton my pants. I try to think sexy thoughts.

Daniel seems both bewildered and thrilled that I'm removing my pants, and before I can do much else he unbuttons his own, revealing boxers with shamrocks all over them. I look away. Not quite ready for clover underwear, I don't think.

We kiss again, but God, I'm ready to stop kissing and just get this over with. Simple act, it's just sex, it's no big deal. Daniel grabs one of my boobs the way someone might catch a baseball. Jonas would probably point and laugh at Daniel's ineptitude; I pretend to like it and reach into my pocket for a condom before twisting out of my jeans entirely.

"What are you doing?" Daniel asks under his breath as he grabs my other boob. Sexy, man. Way sexy. I smile in what I hope is a seductive fashion and hold up the purple condom wrapper. Grape-flavored, apparently.

Daniel's face falls. "Wait, what?"

"Come on," I whisper, slinking one of my legs around him. I press the condom into his hand.

"Wait, Shelby," Daniel says, his voice loud and filled with surprise. "I can't have sex with you."

My mouth drops and my breath escapes. He doesn't want me. What's wrong with him? What's wrong with *me*?

I jerk away from him, and he falls to the floor in surprise.

"Wait—look, sorry, but—"

"What?" I drop the condom. "I'm good enough for second base, but not a home run?"

"Jesus Christ, don't go all crazy. I just don't want to have sex."

"Why not?" I snarl as I stand up and button my pants, trying not to look at the happy rainbows on my underwear.

"I don't know," Daniel mumbles as he grabs his shirt off the futon. "God help me if you got pregnant. My mom would kill me."

"Hence the condom!"

"I don't know, I just...no. Come on, we can make out, maybe even do some other new things...."

"No," I say flatly. Boob squeezing and Cheetos aren't going to get me out of being a thirty-five-year-old virgin, thank you very much. "You know, it's not that big a deal, Daniel. It's just sex."

Daniel looks taken aback for a moment; then angry surprise sweeps over his face like a wave. "So what are you, some kind of slut now?"

"Not hardly," I growl. I grab my purse and leave the condom lying on the floor, where I genuinely hope his mom finds it. I storm out of his room, down the stairs, and toward the front door. I feel stupid, silly, embarrassed, like a failure. I knew this was crazy but—

"Wait!" he yells from upstairs. I freeze. Did he change his mind? "You forgot your DVD." He appears at the bottom of the stairs with the case but doesn't hand it over. "What was this really about, Shelby? You break up with me because you don't like my hobbies, then come over for the first time in ages and want me to have sex with you?"

I sigh. I never explained the Promises to Daniel, and I'm not about to now, much less explain the LOVIN plan. Instead, I settle on, "I just was hoping to lose my virginity finally. You know, I figured I'm getting older, it's about time—"

"Oh my God, are you serious?" Daniel asks. "So...I was your booty call?"

80

"Sort of," I say. "Forget it. I'm going home." I spin on my heel, but Daniel catches my arm.

"Look, Shelby, I'm sorry."

"Whatever," I say. I can hear myself sounding like a bitch, but I'm too frustrated to rein myself in. Daniel opens his mouth again, but I turn and dodge his attempts to stop me. Five minutes later, I'm trudging down the dark street alone. I open up my cell—Ruby has called four times while it was on silent. I dial her back.

"You disappeared! How did it go? Did he argue about the condom? 'Cause guys are sometimes dicks like that, no pun intended."

"He argued about the condom, all right. But then he also argued about the sex in general. So instead of having sex, I'm just walking home."

"What? How is that possible! Did you wear the right panties?"

"Apparently he's still a virgin, and he's not interested."

"Wow. Have you told Jonas?"

"No." I cringe. "And so far the only other guy on my list is Ben Simmons...."

"Is he a Ridgebrook guy?" Ruby asks.

"Yep. Drama kid."

"I think I've heard of him before. Nice guy, kind of sleeps around?"

"That'd be Ben."

"Huh. Kind of ironic, isn't it? That when you were dating Daniel and maybe able to have sex, you weren't really interested, but now that you're interested, it doesn't work out."

"Thanks, Ruby. Being willing but not able is exactly the problem I wanted to reflect on." I sigh.

"Sorry," Ruby says. "I didn't mean it like that. Just that life always seems like that—the minute you want something, you can't have it."

"I guess," I say. "Anyway, call you tomorrow?"

"Sure thing, Shel. Don't worry about it too much, okay?"

"Right."

I trudge down the main road. It's wide enough to walk on, and I'm too irritated to get nervous when cars drive by. Not my safest move, but right now I don't care. I'm too focused on Ruby's words. *Willing but not able*. Such a simple, primal act, and I'm not able to do it. It seemed way easier when losing my virginity was just an idea, a something-that-might-eventually-happen thing instead of a plan. I look up at the moon.

Maybe it's God.

The thought comes to me like a flash, something I didn't mean to think that zips through my head. Maybe God is stepping in and keeping me from having sex. Not that *that* really meshes with that whole free-will thing that they were always telling us to be grateful for at church, but it wouldn't be the first time God—and the church—disappointed me. After all—I prayed. I prayed more than anyone has ever prayed. And it didn't do a thing to help Mom.

I kick a rock in the road, then return my eyes to the sky.

People talk about how they can't believe anyone could deny God's existence, with things like stars and sunsets and circulatory systems and creativity. I understand, though. Because losing your mom is way, way more powerful than stars.

I bring my eyes down to gaze at the road ahead. Maybe God is more like me. Maybe he couldn't save Mom, maybe he couldn't answer the millions of prayers I sent his way, the millions of prayers *everyone* sends his way. Maybe the church, Princess Ball lead sponsor or not, has it all wrong— God's mysteries aren't because we can't understand his plan, but because he doesn't have one at all.

*   *   *   *

Walking home seemed like a better idea when I was storming out of Daniel's house. Two and a half miles later, my feet hurt and I'm incredibly sore from the dance lesson. After much debate, I pull out my phone and call Jonas.

"I thought you were on a hot date tonight," Jonas says.

"Not quite." I sigh. "I'm really sorry to ask, but do you think you could pick me up?"

"Absolutely," Jonas says, his voice now serious. "Are you okay?"

"Oh, yeah. Nothing bad happened. Nothing happened, actually. I'm on the corner of Cypress and Regan Street, over near the drugstore."

"You're *where*?" Jonas asks, and I hear the muffled sounds of him pulling on clothes.

"We can go grab something to eat maybe? I'll buy." I hear the rattling of keys and then the sputtered sound of Lucinda cranking up.

It takes Jonas only fifteen minutes to reach me. He rumbles up with a wary look. I climb in and chuck my purse to the back. The McDonald's smell of Lucinda combined with the sandalwood and fabric softener scent that hangs around Jonas sweeps over me. I inhale. It's a comforting scent, one that drives the lingering Cheetos smell from my head.

"I'd really, really love to know how a sex date with your ex turned into you standing on a street corner," he says. His hair is all stuck up on one side, like he'd been lying on the couch when I called.

I sigh. "Can we go get milk shakes or something?"

Jonas looks down at his T-shirt, which screams of having been in a ball on the floor. "I think Harry's is still open. They have milk shakes, right?"

"I guess." I lean my seat back and close my eyes. "My date bombed," I explain as Lucinda trucks toward the restaurant. "I thought it would be easier."

Jonas glances my way as we pull into the Harry's parking lot. I continue, "I thought Daniel was kind of a sure thing. He was always more than happy to fool around when we were dating."

"So were you, but you wouldn't be hitting him up for sex if you weren't loopholing out of a sex ban," he says.

"True...I guess..." My throat tightens a little. "I guess I figured he'd want to have sex with me regardless."

"Wait," Jonas says, turning the engine off. "Are you worried that he didn't . . . want to?"

"He clearly *didn't* want to, or we wouldn't be having this discussion," I say, sharper than I intended.

"No, he thought he *shouldn't*. Sort of like, 'Oh, I shouldn't eat that candy bar because I'm on a diet' or whatever. It doesn't mean he didn't want the candy bar. Just that he didn't want to . . . uh . . . have sex with the candy bar."

We stare at each other for a moment, then laugh. Jonas hops out of the car and comes around to my side. I reluctantly open my door and step out.

"Does this mean you're on to guy number two?" he asks, his voice a little tense as we walk into Harry's. It's one of those restaurants where they stick up junk on the walls, and I have to duck under the antlers of a jackalope before answering.

"Yep, on to Ben Simmons, I guess — I haven't thought of anyone else for guy number two. At least he isn't likely to miss the hint when I throw myself at him."

"Ben Simmons isn't likely to miss a girl in any regard. . . ."

"Exactly why he'll be perfect," I say. "I just have to figure out a way to . . . you know. Cross his path. We haven't talked in years."

"Welcome to Harry's, home of the Harry Hot Dog. Table for two?" a bright-eyed hostess interrupts us. Jonas nods, and the hostess leads us through a maze of empty tables to a two-person booth tucked away by the kitchen. An old baseball glove and a bat are nailed to the wall beside us.

"You could talk to Anna," Jonas says as he browses the menu. "She hangs out with him from time to time."

"Didn't she say she made out with him at a party?" I ask.

Jonas pauses to order us both chocolate milk shakes when the waitress arrives. "Yeah," he finally answers me. "But it was a long time ago."

"I guess I could ask her." Anna isn't someone I really talk to outside of school. Surely there's an easier way to meet Ben.

"Here," Jonas says. "I have her number."

I'm surprised, but then again, Jonas has always been a bigger fan of Anna's than I have. I copy the number into my phone, finishing just as our shakes arrive. I'm not as hungry as I thought—I stir my milk shake till the whipped cream vanishes. *Ben Simmons. Who'd have thought?* I didn't really want to have sex with Daniel, but I remember that back when we were dating it had crossed my mind. So it didn't seem too crazy to have sex with him. But Ben? I've never wanted Ben, not really.

"Are you okay?" Jonas asks.

"Yeah." I shrug. "Just thinking about Ben. I never really pictured how I wanted my first time to be, you know? But now that I'm trying to have it, I feel like I'm giving up some fantasy that never even existed to begin with."

"Like what?" Jonas asks cautiously.

I flush a little. "I don't know. With someone I love, I guess. I never thought I'd do the whole wait-till-marriage thing, but I think I wanted it to be with someone I cared about."

Jonas sighs and sits back in the booth. "You can always try to talk to your dad again," he suggests, and I'm grateful that he knows me well enough not to try to persuade me to break the Promises.

I shake my head. "I don't know. I'm afraid that if I fight it too hard, he'll get the wrong idea and think I'm shacking up nightly. Besides, it's not the sex itself that bothers me, so much as having to make a choice about my virginity so soon. I didn't realize I had secretly planned how I wanted my first time," I say, trying to make it a joke. "I mean, you probably have a secret plan for how you want it to go, too. Think about it."

Jonas grins, but his ears turn a little red. "I guess I do. And mine doesn't involve Ben Simmons, either," he says, and I laugh. There's a moment's silence in which I zone in on the cherry at the bottom of my milk shake glass.

For Jonas's sake, I change the subject and let him show me his most recent list—colleges he wants to apply to, the ones that need extra admissions essays marked with a messily drawn star.

An hour later, we're pulling into my driveway. "Thanks for picking me up," I tell Jonas as I swing my feet out of the car.

"Don't mention it," he says. "What's gone and what's past help should be past grief."

"I don't know that quote," I answer, frowning.

"*The Winter's Tale*. Not one of Shakespeare's most popular plays. But seriously—Daniel's loss."

I smile, then step back and shut the car door.

Inside, Dad is planted in front of the television, sound asleep. It's almost eleven, so whatever show he's watching has long gone off to make way for a Super Shammy infomercial. I try to shut the door quietly, but he sits up anyway.

"Shelby? What time is it?"

"Eleven," I say. "Sorry I woke you up."

Dad looks at me carefully, his expression a mix of curiosity and confusion. I don't really have a set curfew, but eleven is later than usual. He wants to ask me where I was, I can tell, but he won't, because he never has before—it'd break the routine. Even so, the weight of the night's events is heavy in my mind, and something that tastes oddly like guilt forces me to look at the floor. Dad exhales.

"I wrote you a note," he says, pointing the remote to turn off the TV. I grab a slip of paper off the counter: *Cake Tasting Friday at Noon!*

"There's a cake tasting?" I ask. "Like, at the grocery store?"

"No," Dad says, shoving his hands in his pockets. "It's a wedding cake bakery. Sweet Cakes or Sweet Caking or something. I can go alone, if you want," he adds quickly.

"Uh, no. I'll go. No problem."

We stare at each other for a moment longer.

"Well... good night," Dad says.

"Night."

24 days before

I did not anticipate my Thursday going this way. I wanted to spend the day lying around, trying to get over what happened with Daniel, and getting up the nerve to call Anna about Ben Simmons. All that accompanied by at least one quart of ice cream.

But no. I thought Dad was going to some sort of planning session with the rest of the Princess Ball committee and just wanted me to come. It isn't until we get to the church that Dad springs it on me: I'm here to talk with a group of Princess Ball attendees. And the pastor. They call it a Princess Meeting. I call it Personal Hell.

I mean, forget the fact that I pretty much always hate talking to pastors — they have this way of sneaking God into the conversation. You'll be talking about something mundane, like creamed corn, and all of a sudden creamed corn is a symbol of how God loves you. But pastors aside, I just don't want to be around the other Princess Ball attendees. From what I've heard at school and seen at the waltz lesson, most of them are good girls, sweet girls, girls who have "it" figured out, whatever it is. They've got straight As and flawless makeup and whole families and probably golden retrievers.

Hanging out with those kinds of girls feels like showing up to a party naked. No, they don't laugh and point—they swarm to help me, include me, talk to me, when all I really want to do is run home and find a shirt.

I sigh as I walk down the church hallway; the sound of thirty-some girls in full talking frenzy pours down the corridor. I take a deep breath and turn the corner into the classroom.

The room is the preschool Sunday school room, covered in craft projects and bright posters. I recognize almost everyone, either from school or from my youth group days. I take a seat as far away from everyone else as possible, which is tricky given that the chairs are arranged in a messy circle. Mona Banks waves from the other side of the room; I pretend not to notice, but she heads my way regardless.

"Hey, Shelby!" Mona calls.

"Hi, Mona," I say, without an attempt to match her enthusiasm. She slides into the chair next to me and flips her hair over her shoulder.

"So, I was talking to some friends about the ball and how you get to plan it while we were working on this Habitat for Humanity house this week. They were so jealous!"

"Things are going pretty good. We have a cake tasting on Friday."

"Oh, I'm jealous! I also heard about this thing that my cousin did at her city's father-daughter-princess-ball thing; I bet you already know about it. With the roses?"

"Haven't heard of it," I say, which Mona interprets as "Tell me more!"

"Well, everyone gets a big white rose and they take your picture in your dress with it, handing it to your father," Mona explains, twisting her hair around her fingers.

"Sounds...showy."

"Yeah, that's sort of the point, isn't it?" Mona says. She waves to a few other youth group girls, who venture our way. "A big show about being good daughters and whatever?"

I laugh a little. "Right. Right."

Mona laughs, then lowers her voice. "Though I have to admit, it's kind of funny. The questionnaires and the whole bonding thing...like they think this dance will make me go talk to my dad about stuff. It's like those drug promises they make you sign in elementary school—do they really think those work?"

I stare at Mona for a moment. Mona Banks? Perfect Girl poster child? "What do you mean?" I ask.

Mona giggles and her friends lean in to listen. "I mean, come on. It's just a dance. Those vows they added in are so stupid, but...they make my dad happy, so whatever, I guess...."

Right. You aren't bound by promises. This is just a joke to you. I almost feel betrayed—these girls look like the cast of one of those cheery don't-do-drugs videos they make you watch in health class, and have everyone believing it. But they aren't. They aren't perfect. I shouldn't be jealous of Mona and her total, complete faith after all, because it's not real—she's like a math problem, the kind where you got the right answer but didn't show any of your work. Mona is the right answer, but she didn't get there by going through anything difficult, by questioning God, by doubting. She landed there by playing a part, but she's never done the work.

I swallow. I'm still jealous.

I'm about to respond when the pastor steps into the room, all smiles and shampoo-commercial hair.

"Ladies, ladies, thank you so much for coming today," the pastor says, sitting down in a chair by the door. "It's nice to see so many people participating in the Princess Ball— we've had to split you into three groups to have these little sessions! Anyhow, most of you know me—a few of you don't. I'm Pastor Ryan, and I'm here to talk to you a little bit about what the Princess Ball is really all about."

Everyone smiles at him. He leans back in the chair, as if deciding where to begin. It's a convincing ruse, except I'm pretty certain no pastor has ever entered a room without knowing what he'll say. Prepared speeches are kind of in the job description.

"The Princess Ball is all about solidifying your relationship with your father. Sometimes it's easy to overlook the ways your father shows you he cares about you. I'd like to go around the room and have everyone tell us about a way your father shows you he loves you."

I wonder if they'd notice me leaping out the window—I stare at it longingly as the first girl starts. She talks about her dad's paying for her to attend the local private school. The next one talks about "family night" where they play board games. One cites her father's always asking about her day. Another one says they make breakfast together on Saturdays. It's coming around to me. *Come on, Shelby, think of something, make something up, anything.* I try to formulate an answer, something that girl on the cover of the Princess Ball pamphlet would say. "Shelby?" Pastor Ryan says.

All eyes on me.

I freeze. "Um...my father..." My face flushes as much from guilt as embarrassment—I mean, my dad and I aren't exactly making pancake breakfasts, but it's not like he's a terrible guy or something.

"How about...the way your father takes a very active role in the community so that it's a better environment for you to grow up in?" Pastor Ryan suggests.

"Yes. That," I say automatically. It's only after the words leave my mouth that I consider what Pastor Ryan just said. Is that why Dad would medal in the Volunteer Olympics? For me? Maybe—I don't think he was in the Organic Produce League for my benefit, but I can't justify why else he'd head up the Princess Ball planning committee if it wasn't for me. I guess I've never really thought about it.

I dwell on that as the remaining girls answer, and Pastor Ryan talks about ways we can show that we love and appreciate our fathers. It's mostly stuff I do for Promise One anyway, so I tune him out, until he says—

"Living a pure life. Free from drugs, free from alcohol—for now, at least, and in moderation when you're old enough—and free from sex until you've made your marriage vows." He pauses, looks around the room—I notice more than a few girls dodging his eyes. He continues, "Your purity is the most precious gift God gave you. And God gave you a father to guide you and help you keep that gift until it's time for you to start a new life with your husband."

God gave me a mother, too, and look how that turned out, I think bitterly. I'm instantly sorry—not to God, or anything, but to Mom. Using her name in a mental comeback to Pastor Ryan feels like I've cheapened her.

Pastor Ryan's tone darkens. "But sometimes, the idea of giving away your purity sounds very tempting, doesn't it? Sometimes people will tempt you. The devil tempted Eve—I'm sure you all know the story from one place or another. The devil wanted Eve to give up another one of God's precious gifts, the Garden of Eden. And Eve was tempted. She couldn't resist, and she sacrificed God's gifts. And in the end...Eve felt shame. She knew she wasted God's gift, and she was disgraced."

Pastor Ryan pretends not to notice a girl who is too busy texting to listen to him. "You're lucky, though, all of you. Not only can you learn from Eve's mistakes, but by becoming closer to your father through the Princess Ball, you'll have help resisting temptation. You'll never have to know what it's like to feel like you've let God down."

Holy shit. And I mean "holy" in the most sincere way.

I look around—some of the girls are paying rapt attention, some are ignoring him, and a few others look as irritated by the whole speech as I am. I think of my younger self, back when I still went to church—I had preschool in this exact room. I remember being told by pastors, elders, little old ladies, and well-meaning church friends about how important it was to pray for my mom. How God would do what was best. How God loved me. And here they are again, telling me I might let God down?

God let *me* down. I raise my hand.

"Yes, Shelby?" Pastor Ryan asks.

"So what about Adam?" I ask, trying to appear eager and knowledge-seeking instead of annoyed and bitter.

"I'm sorry, what?" Pastor Ryan asks, bright-eyed. My nerves spike.

"I was just thinking," I say. "What about Adam? Didn't he taste the fruit, too?"

"Yes..." Pastor Ryan nods and leans back in his chair, a studious look on his face. "What about him?"

"So, um, if he tried the fruit...shouldn't guys be having Princess Balls, too? Or Prince Balls, I guess?" I didn't mean the question to be *entirely* sarcastic, nor did I mean to say "prince balls," but I really want to know why the hell guys aren't stuck in this tomb of eternal virginity with us.

"Well, Shelby, luckily there just don't seem to be as many temptations in the world for young men as there are for young ladies," Pastor Ryan says, smiling. "But I think instead of focusing on why we haven't invited boys to the ball, we should focus on why we have invited *you*. It's so important that fathers and daughters understand their roles in each other's lives. I hope you leave today's session with the sense that you and your father together have the armor to protect you from falling victim."

I want to yell at him. I want to fight. Why does he always have to smile? Why is he always so calm? I wish he'd scream at me, so I could justify screaming back. It isn't fair that he always has an answer, yet it's never an answer that satisfies me. It isn't fair that he and the rest of them can say, "God has a plan" and drop the issue, while I'm left wondering what the hell God's plan is and why he won't let me in on it. It isn't fair that half the girls in this room don't care about the vows, and the other half are Perfect Girls and Perfect Daughters and Perfect Believers who would never break them anyway.

It

isn't

fair.

But instead of saying that, I stare at the poorly executed paintings of Jesus that line the room, letting my sizzling temper cool as Pastor Ryan talks. They're big, blocky portraits of a porcelain-skinned, dark-haired Jesus cuddling lambs, offering a hand to children, waving an arm to create a rainbow. Picture Book Jesus, the one who's easy to have faith in.

Mom never really read Bible stories to me. In fact, she never seemed all that into church—and before she got sick, Dad took me with him more out of habit than faith. So at home, she stuck to the classics: *If You Give a Mouse a Cookie*, *Goodnight Moon*, *The Story of Ferdinand*, and, at least once every few months, *A Little Princess*. Sometimes, in a bookless situation, she made up stories; other times we sang—my favorite song was that "Going On a Bear Hunt" thing.

We're goin' on a bear hunt!
We're gonna catch a big one!
We're not scared!

I'd repeat each line after her, making it a strange duet. It was the same every time—you come to tall grass, a wide river, a dark cave, and you always *can't go over it! Can't go under it! We'll have to go through it!*

Mom and I would go through the tall grass or wide river or dark cave or any number of obstacles with big, dramatic hand motions. It didn't matter where we were—restaurant, waiting room, bookstore—she was never embarrassed to be going through a wide river with her giggly daughter. Dad would laugh and smile and act enthused by our bear-hunt tale.

It always ended the same way—we see the imaginary bear, then run back through the river, the cave, the tall grass. We wound up where we started, safe and together and happy, even if our hunt was fruitless.

I narrow my eyes at Picture Book Jesus. So much easier to believe in when I was little and he was just a nice man in a nice story. Just like it was easy to believe in a bear at the end of a make-believe hunt.

But now Jesus isn't just a nice man. He's part of the force that stole my mom. He's the being I can never catch to blame, to hate, to believe in, to grab onto, because whenever I get close I have to run back through the cave, the river, the grass, and start my journey all over again. And I have to do it all without a mom to guide me.

The only thing I leave the session with is a sense of certainty that Eve made a fair trade by eating that fruit. She traded paradise for knowledge. She wanted to know the truth about evil, about God, about sex, just like I do.

Way to go, Eve.

Pastor Ryan stands at the doorway, giving everyone high fives as we leave the classroom. His hand rests on mine a bit longer than everyone else's, and there's pity in his eyes. I ignore it and walk out.

Maybe he's right. Maybe Eve did feel worthless for betraying God—maybe I'll feel worthless if I have sex. But at least that way, God would be coming through the way everyone predicted. At least that way, I would know that the church's version of God isn't just a picture-book fantasy.

Which means I'd finally be able to confront the glorious, giving, benevolent God for not saving Mom.

23 days before

The bakery isn't far from Flying Biscuit. It doesn't look like much—a converted house sandwiched between two law-yers' offices. A tiny, cake-shaped bell tinkles as we walk in.

The shop is heavy with the scent of potpourri, a thick, sweet smell that sticks to the sides of my lungs. Dad adjusts his tie and coughs uncomfortably. I want to tell him that I don't think a little cough is going to clear that odor from his throat, but instead I just shrug when our eyes accidentally meet.

"Hi! Welcome to Sweet Bakin' Cakes!" a woman's voice shouts above the sound of crackly classical music. I have no idea where this mysterious woman is—it's impossible to see to the back of the shop because of the maze of giant cakes that adorn tables throughout. They're huge and look like they've been carved rather than baked, boasting displays of perfectly smooth frosting and silk flowers. Most are white or ivory wedding cakes with tiny, poorly painted brides and grooms on the top, but there are a few that are more unusual—one that looks like it's been pleated, one covered in polka dots, even one with paisley patterns drawn all over it. I'm staring at a cake with plaid icing when the woman appears, swishing out from behind a sign that says *Let them eat cake* in lavender bubble letters.

The woman might also be made out of cake; her eyes and lips are covered in pink makeup that has a silver, frosted undertone, and her skin is layered with so much foundation that she must have spread it on with a frosting knife. She walks forward, ankles twisting dangerously in hot-pink heels. I glance at my dad and catch a hint of amusement on his face.

"Hi," Dad says, reaching out to shake her well-manicured hand. "You must be Wanda? I called earlier—we're here to sample cakes for the Princess Ball?"

"Oh yes! I love Princess Ball time," Wanda cries, clasping her hands together. "Follow me, follow me."

Dad almost runs into a seven-tiered wedding cake with pink frosting circles all over it, and I have to keep ducking under balloon displays. Wanda doesn't seem to notice our struggle, however, and we finally reach the back of the shop. Windows overlook the parking lot, and three tiny café tables are set up and piled high with thick photo albums.

"Just have a seat here," Wanda says, pulling out one of the café chairs, a white cast-iron contraption with a tiny seat and ornately curved back. I lower myself into it; Dad sinks into the other. While Wanda sorts through the photo albums, mumbling to herself, Dad and I desperately try to arrange ourselves so we aren't sitting quite so close to each other. The kitchen table at home is vast, especially since the space that used to hold three now holds only two; this tiny little table is meant for two tiny people, not two average-sized people and a rather plump woman.

"Now, I have twelve different varieties of cake and icing combinations for you to sample, and then we'll select the style of cake," Wanda informs us. She drops most of the photo albums on the floor with a resounding *crack*; Dad and I jump. Undeterred, Wanda slides the remaining album toward us. "Just start skimming through those. These are all our larger cakes, because this has to feed...how many is it, again?"

"We're anticipating about two hundred," Dad says. Wanda's eyes fill with joy, and I think she's clenching her teeth to keep from shouting.

"It's wonderful to see young ladies excited about a dance with their fathers!" Wanda says. Dad and I share forced smiles. "Anyhow, look through those while I go grab the first few samples."

And then she leaves, deftly maneuvering through the cakes before vanishing.

Dad taps his fingers for a moment, then slides his thumb under the photo album's cover. The cellophane covering the photos crackles. I lean over, trying to look interested.

He turns a page. The air-conditioning kicks on, and the silk flowers on the nearest cake begin to tremble.

"This one is very...yellow," Dad says, pointing to a cake that's a highlighter shade. Its tiers are oddly shaped and it's covered in violet flowers, so it looks like something out of a Dr. Seuss book.

"Yeah," I agree, and when I can't think of anything else to say, I force a small laugh. This seems to ease Dad a little bit; he chuckles when we turn to a massive cake that's covered in *Star Wars* figures drawn in icing.

"That's actually kind of cool," I say, turning the book so it faces me.

"I know. What would the rest of the committee do if we showed up at the ball with this?" Dad asks.

"May the force be with them," I say, relieved when Dad laughs at my terrible joke. I continue, "What if we got that highlighter cake, but then had them put *Star Wars* drawings on it?"

Dad laughs and turns the page, then another. "And... maybe the topper from this cake?" he suggests, pointing to a cake topper of a couple dressed up as clowns.

"We could even have Darth Vader and Leia on top of the cake. You know, father and daughter?" I add.

Dad cracks up, his laughter brighter and louder than it's been in years. He winds down from the fit and shakes his head, trying to regain control. "That'd be perfect—I didn't know you'd watched the original *Star Wars*."

"It's impossible not to. They're on TV every weekend," I say with a shrug.

"We should watch them sometime," Dad says quickly, and when the words leave his mouth, it's like he remembers the suggestion should be more awkward. "I mean, if you want."

"Sure," I answer, and flip the page of the cake book

again. Wanda soon comes bustling back in, pushing a black cast-iron tea cart. It's loaded with white plates that have miniature cakes, all immaculately iced and identical in size and shape. The poor man's version of the dolled-up monstrosities outside.

"Hmm...where to begin..." Wanda says, waving a hand over her display of cakes. "Ah, yes!" She grins at me. "The princess cake! Seems like a good place to start for the Princess Ball! What was your name again, hon?"

"Shelby."

"Ah, well, how about I call you Princess Shelby, then?" Wanda giggles, clearly not reading the look of horror on my face. "Anyhoo, this is our princess cake—white cake with cream-cheese frosting. That's a creamy white, because we leave the egg yolks in. We can also do this in an almond flavor. Fairly popular for the Princess Ball, but keep in mind it's just an option." Wanda puts the plate in the center of the table and divides it into three slices with a silver knife. She then hands my father and me forks; we tentatively pick off tiny slivers of cake. I expect it'll taste like the heavy perfume Wanda is wearing and tense my jaw as I take a bite.

It's the most delicious thing I've ever tasted. Seriously. The princess cake half melts in my mouth; the soft, buttery flavor of the cake blends seamlessly with the tangy cream-cheese icing. Its richness makes the chill from the air conditioner fade, like it's warming me from the inside out. My dad's eyes widen in matching delight; we make brief eye contact before greedily jumping back for a second taste. That seems to thrill Wanda; she loads up her own fork, smearing her bright pink lipstick when she shovels a second bite into her mouth. My dad abandons all manners and sinks his fork into a piece so large he has to take a moment to balance it. I take a page out of his book and do the same when I go back for a third piece.

I've seen enough episodes of those wedding-planning shows with Ruby to know that I'm not really supposed to eat the entire slice. Nonetheless, my dad, Wanda, and I nearly decimate the princess cake. Which is when Wanda pulls out the Black Forest cake — devil's food cake with cream-cheese frosting and cherries. Then the Italian wedding cake, which has amaretto frosting and almonds baked right in. Then German chocolate, then red velvet, then something decorated with raspberries, then something iced with a fudge ganache and sprinkled with coconut. Wanda brings out bottles of water as we continue on to lemon-raspberry torte and orange buttercream.

By the time we hit the last few, which are basics — chocolate/chocolate, chocolate/vanilla, and vanilla/vanilla — Dad and I are leaning back in our chairs, crumbs decorating our shirts and icing smudges on our fingers. Wanda is still going strong, sampling the chocolate/chocolate with the same vigor that she did the princess cake. I swallow the rest of my water, trying to ignore the rush of sugar that's coursing through my veins.

"So what do we think?" Wanda asks, the same question she asked after each and every sample cake — all twelve of them.

104

"Um...well..." Dad says, glancing to me.

I shrug. "I liked the first one, honestly. If we go with any of the really fancy stuff, someone will probably be allergic or hate chocolate or whatever."

"The first one? The princess cake?" Wanda asks. She eats another forkful of chocolate/chocolate, seemingly disappointed—I get the impression that the princess cake is the least expensive of the set. "And what pattern?"

I remember the yellow *Star Wars* clown cake and giggle; I get the feeling Dad is thinking of it, too, since I catch him staring at his fork and stifling a secret smile aimed at me.

"We may need to think on that," Dad finally says. "Unless there was something you liked, Shelby?" He asks it with a twinkle in his eyes, daring me to order it.

"No," I answer, holding in a snicker. "I'm good."

"Right, then, Wanda, I'll just give you a call after we've thought on it for a few days."

"Keep in mind, we can make just about anything," Wanda says as we rise and move to the door. Avoiding the giant cake displays was hard enough the first time, but now that we're stuffed and sluggish, it's near impossible. We somehow make it to the car without sending too many confections teetering on their stands.

"Who knew there were so many types of cake? I thought it was just...cake. Chocolate, vanilla...cake," Dad says as we back out of the Sweet Bakin' Cakes parking lot.

"When you said Princess Ball, I figured something less like a wedding," I say. I instantly worry I've said too much—

truth is, planning this thing hasn't been quite as bad as I anticipated. I'd hate to have made it this far without wounding Dad's feelings only to crush them now.

"You and me both, actually," Dad answers, and it makes me smile. "You know how much I hate suits...."

"Speaking of," I add as we zip past the rows of strip malls that flank Sweet Bakin' Cakes, "do you think I can wear my old winter formal dress to this thing?" I cast away a stab of spite for Mona Banks, all dressed up to give an insincere vow.

"That light green one?" Dad asks, and I'm ashamed to realize it surprises me he remembers. Dad looks over at me as we come to a stoplight, and I nod. "I think you're supposed to wear white. Maybe they've changed the rule, though. But you can buy something new, Shelby. I don't mind paying."

"Yeah..." I try not to cringe at the memory of picking out my homecoming dress. Ruby was out of town, so I ended up letting the saleslady pick it out because I just wanted to get out of there. Hearing "This one really minimizes your butt" seventeen times in an hour was not a pleasant experience. The light turns green, but Dad doesn't stop looking at me; it's like he's analyzing, reading something for the first time.

"Maybe we can figure something out," he says, finally urging the car forward. "If you don't like dress shopping. That's it, right? You don't like dress shopping?"

"You've nailed it," I answer, smiling a little. "I can pull something together, though."

Dad nods, but I can practically see little gears turning in his head.

There's not too much left of the day by the time we get home. I watch TV for a while, too full to move, then eventually entertain the notion of cleaning my room. When I toss an armload of clothes into my closet, I uncover the ball questionnaire.

I lift the paper, still folded unevenly, and open it. Same stupid, annoying questions. I scrounge up a pencil from my barely visible carpet and write in, "We both enjoy edible *Star Wars* memorabilia." I grin and look at question seven as I lower myself to my bed.

7. What is your favorite memory of your father?

My favorite memory of Dad. Huh. I tap my pencil on the paper for a few moments. The trouble is, I don't really have any memories of my dad. I have memories of my mom in which Dad was present, but they're undeniably memories of her. My dad and I are merely players in the scenes, the ensemble of a grand performance that was her life. Everything from my childhood involves her, somehow, with my dad tagging along for the ride. I think back as far as I can go, but no, even my first memory is of *her* on my fifth birthday, helping me decorate the lopsided cake she made me. I vaguely remember Dad leaning over me as I blew out the candles, but I remember Mom's arm around me, her face close to mine. I remember the way she smelled, the way she spoke, the way her hair brushed my shoulders. But he was just in the background— I'm not even positive about where he was standing.

The memories mostly exclude Dad all the way up to the point when Mom got sick, and even then my "alone time" with my dad was only a result of her illness. We were still wrapped up in her needs, her wants, her time. What was left of it, anyway.

I sigh and lie back on my pillows. There has to be something, though, something with just Dad and me. Or *more* Dad and me, even, since cutting Mom out of the picture altogether seems pretty impossible.

The french fries.

Yes, yes, the french fries. I close my eyes, trying to remember the scene perfectly before I write it down. It's tied up with Mom, of course, but still...it was when Mom had gotten so sick, they'd turned to "experimental" treatment, which even at ten I understood meant "we're practically just giving her vitamins and seeing what happens." It was near the end, though of course I didn't totally realize that. My mom had taken my dad and me to the fall carnival every year before she got sick, and she begged Dad to take me alone since she couldn't go. I didn't *want* to go with him, and I suspect he didn't really want to leave her bedside to go with me, but we were both so desperate to make her happy that we agreed.

"Bring me something back," she said with a weak wave as we left the hospital room, bundled up in scarves and hats.

"Like what? A stuffed animal?" Dad asked. I could see

the worry in his eyes as he tried to figure out what monumental task of a carnival game he'd have to accomplish to win a giant teddy bear.

"French fries. They have those french fries at that stall. All they sell is french fries. Just bring me back some of those."

"Jenny, they'll be cold by the time we get back with them. I could bring you some cotton candy, maybe? It'll keep."

But no, she insisted on french fries. So after we walked around the carnival for an hour, rode the Ferris wheel more out of obligation than desire, and tried to ignore the sights of little girls with their beautiful, healthy, perfect mothers, we stopped at the french fries stall. Dad bought a box of french fries and asked for extra aluminum foil to wrap them up tightly. By the time we got back to the hospital, they were all cold, and Mom was so sick she could eat only one.

But still. I remember watching Dad carefully wrap the french fries, and how simply *nice* I thought it was that he was getting them, knowing they'd be cold and mushy by the time we got back to the hospital. There was something beautiful in someone trying to purchase happiness for a dying woman via a three-dollar box of french fries. I remember hoping that one day someone would buy me french fries if that's all I wanted, even if he knew they'd be no good in the end.

I remember understanding what love really was. It didn't hurt; it didn't ignore your prayers, didn't seem to not care that your mom was dying. It didn't leave you wondering what you did wrong. Love tried to make you happy, even if it was useless. Love would do anything to make you happy.

I can't write all that down. Even if I wanted to, I'm not sure I could find the words. Instead, I just scribble down "French fries day" and figure if Dad wants me to explain when we go over the questionnaires, I can. Or maybe he'll remember french fries day on his own.

How could he forget it?

22 days before

I'm still thinking about cakes the next day—probably because the sugar high doesn't show signs of wearing off for a few weeks at best. I head to Flying Biscuit to meet Jonas for lunch. Apparently he's been there all day continuing to work on college admissions essays, because he doesn't know how to use his summer vacation for anything other than evil. I barge in the door and glance toward my and Jonas's normal booth.

To my surprise, sitting to Jonas's right is Anna Clemens. She looks up at me and waves with a big grin on her face. I nod and wait for Jonas's eyes to rise and meet mine. He shrugs, and I wind through tables and empty chairs to take a seat across from him in the booth. The table is covered in papers with college logos at the top, but very little work seems to have actually been done—the legal pad beside Jonas's plate is empty. I step toward their table, but Ruby suddenly steps in front of me, cutting me off.

"I got you an early birthday present!"

"My birthday isn't till November," I remind her.

"A really, really early birthday present, then. Jeffery,

cover my table for a second?" she calls across the restaurant, and he nods. I raise my eyebrows as Ruby ducks behind the hostess station, then pops back up with a Victoria's Secret bag.

"They're not the expensive ones—do you have any idea how much nice lace naughty panties cost? I was floored. Especially considering they're made to end up *on* the floor."

I peer into the bag, where a pair of black panties with little pink bows on them rests amid tissue paper.

"For Ben, you know. So you can knock this thing out. See, I'm a supportive friend, even if I don't keep your list!" she says.

"Much appreciated," I say, grinning. I look back at Jonas and Anna. "So has she been here all day?" Flying Biscuit is sort of my and Jonas's and Ruby's place, I thought, and I'm surprised that Anna's presence feels so . . . strange.

"Yep. Why?" she asks.

"No reason." I shrug and walk over to the booth. I try to hide the pink bag from view, although I can tell from Jonas's expression that Ruby has already told him—and probably shown him—her pity gift to me. Anna grins as I sit down.

"Hey, Shel!" she says. "How's your summer going?"

"Pretty good, yours?" I ask.

"I got invited to the drama department's year-wrap party next Saturday," Anna says with a shrug, though her eyes are sparkling with delight.

"The wrap party? Who goes to that?" Jonas asks with a note of concern. "Wrap parties" are the drama department's way of throwing giant alcohol fests. I don't know why they need an excuse—the cheerleaders certainly don't—but they always call them wrap parties.

"Everyone, especially since Kell was in the spring play," Anna says gleefully. Kell was a cheerleader who somehow got into the musical-theater class. She managed to bring a huge crowd to the spring play's opening night, despite the fact that she had a nonspeaking part and kept waving at people from the stage.

"Huh," Jonas says, and dives into his grits.

"Will—" I hesitate. "Will Ben Simmons be there?" Jonas's eyes dart up at me.

"It's at Ben Simmons's house, actually," Anna says. "I think he's providing all the beer. Or his parents are or something." Ben's parents are famous at Ridgebrook for being of the "If you want to drink, I'd rather you do it in the house" mentality.

"Do you think I could tag along?" I ask carefully. Best to play it casual. If I get too eager, Anna will think I'll embarrass her and I'll never get the invite.

"Um…" Anna studies me, and I can tell she's playing through various scenes in which I might kill her fragile popularity. "I guess," she finally says. "Why? Wait, didn't you ask me about Ben Simmons during finals week?" she says, a sly grin tugging at the corners of her mouth.

I lie. "I'm just a little interested in him. I thought maybe I could talk to him at the party or something."

"Talking isn't his strong point," Anna says, giggling and shimmying her shoulders a bit.

"Well, that, too," I add, but I can feel my cheeks turning a little bit red.

"I so don't want to hear this conversation," Jonas says.

"Ah, sorry," Anna says, though her giggly voice continues. "Anyway, Shel, just give me a call on Saturday and I'll swing by your house and pick you up if you want. Do you know what you're going to wear?"

"Not really."

"Maybe I'll bring over some of my clothes just in case," Anna says, a warm smile trying to disguise the "your clothes might suck" expression underneath it.

"Sounds good," I answer as Anna slides out of the booth, then heads to the bathroom.

"What's she doing here?" I ask as she disappears.

"I do hang out with people other than you and Ruby, you know," Jonas says, smiling. "I mean... not often. And not many people. But sometimes I do."

"All girls, though, I've noticed," Ruby teases, swinging by the table to hand me a drink. She flashes a grin as she walks away.

"Not exactly a bad thing," Jonas calls after her.

"You should come to the party, too," I suggest when Jonas turns back to me. He raises his eyebrows.

"Not my scene. Also, rumor is that if you get too close to Ben Simmons, you wake up ten years in the future in a community college production of *Oklahoma!*"

"He's not that bad."

"Bad? No. It's hard to have personality traits as intense

as 'bad' after crushing all those beer cans on your head." I roll my eyes but laugh anyway.

"It's the only way," I say when I see Anna coming back from the bathroom.

"I'm not debating that," Jonas says. "But that doesn't mean I want to think about you and Ben Simmons if I can avoid it."

I wouldn't say it out loud, but to be honest, I don't really want to think about me and Ben Simmons, either—especially when Anna slides back in beside Jonas and I remember that she and Ben hooked up once. I'll be kissing the same lips Anna Clemens did. That's just wrong.

But what choice do I have?

20 days before

Monday morning, when I trudge downstairs in my pajamas, my breath catches in my throat.

Sitting in our dilapidated living room is my dad's sister, my aunt Kaycee. She's wearing a short skirt and a cowboy hat. Because, you know, she's going to wrangle some cattle in those designer alligator-print sandals. Her face is caked in makeup and bears evidence of at least one or two plastic surgeries, and I'm pretty sure the itty-bitty designer handbag she's carrying probably cost more than most cars.

"Hey, Shel! Are you ready to go dress shopping?" she near-shouts.

"Oh no," I say before I can stop myself.

"Shelby? Is that you?" I hear my dad call from the kitchen over the sound of running water. He steps out, drying an ancient plastic cup that says *Myrtle Beach* on the side. He's grinning. "I thought Kaycee could go dress shopping with you today. You know, to help you out and stuff." His good intentions, clearly based on our conversation post–cake tasting, are laid out on his face. Part of me wants to slap them away. Especially when Kaycee bounces on her heels like a person in her teens, not forties. *Promise One*, I chant to myself. *Love and listen to Dad. Promise One.* I have to do it.

"Come on, girl! It'll be a blast. We can even get smoothies afterward—I'm on day four of my carb-sugar-fat cleanse so I'm allowed *anything* with organic strawberries now!" Kaycee says enthusiastically. Dad gives me a hopeful look. This Princess Ball is making Promise One very, very hard to keep.

"Mind if I bring some friends along?" I ask.

"Sure! The more the merrier," Kaycee says. Is she drunk? I think she might be drunk. Surely no one is this happy about dress shopping without some sort of alcoholic assistance.

I run upstairs and dial Ruby and Jonas.

I have a feeling the desperation in my voice persuaded them to hurry, because within thirty minutes they've arrived together in Lucinda. Soon after, Ruby is applying her eyeliner in the back of Kaycee's sedan as we race toward Four Corners Mall.

"Be careful with that makeup, Reba," Kaycee says warily. "I just got this whole thing detailed."

"Ruby," I correct her. Kaycee doesn't seem to hear me. When we exit the car, Kaycee glances back at the seat Ruby was sitting in, as if she expects to find giant streaks of Maybelline on them.

"Shoot, someone hold my keys? They don't fit in my clutch," Kaycee says, holding up the tiny sparkly purse she's carrying. Ruby rolls her eyes and allows Kaycee to drop the keys, complete with key chains bearing beads, rubber ducks, and *New Orleans 05!*, into her palm.

Sending Aunt Kaycee to pick out a dress for a virgin ball seems a little bit like sending a wolf to host a sheep's birthday party. She sweeps into the formal-gown section of Macy's like the grand duchess of style and begins pulling dresses off racks so quickly that soon she's hidden behind a mountain of taffeta. Ruby and Jonas look scared, like I've just led them into a war zone.

"That's the eleventh pink dress she's picked up," Jonas mutters in amazement. The store is organized by color and, much to Kaycee's delight, seems to have an extensive collection of dresses befitting Tropical Barbie.

"All the girls in the brochure were wearing white, weren't they? Didn't your mom wear white to it?" Ruby asks as Kaycee finds the turquoise dresses with a delighted squeal.

"Kaycee doesn't like white," I say. "She *and* her bridesmaids wore sunshine yellow to her second wedding. But I'll admit, I do sorta want to see everyone's faces when I show up in lime green."

"Good point," Jonas says. "Make sure you take a picture for me. Hey, do you think if we formed a 'Ban Kaycee Reaver from Ridgebrook' committee, your dad would join it?"

I smile just a little and answer, "I'll happily be committee president either way —"

"Shelby! Here, they're gonna put these in a room for you. Go ahead and start trying them on while I grab a few more!" Kaycee shouts from across the racks of dresses. I give her a thumbs-up and giggle with Jonas and Ruby as soon as Kaycee turns her back.

"Just give me whichever monstrosity you end up with," Ruby suggests. "I can probably make it wearable."

"Shelby? Hey!" a voice cries out. I turn to see Mona Banks heading toward me, detouring around circular racks of clothing. It takes her ages to actually reach me.

"Hey, Mona," Jonas says.

"And Ruby, right?" Mona says, nodding in Ruby's direction. "I haven't seen you in forever!"

"It's a shame, isn't it?" Ruby answers, though I'm not sure if she means the amount of time they haven't seen each other is a shame, or the fact that they have seen each other again is a shame. From the snarky expression on Ruby's face, I'd say the latter.

"Shopping for your ball gown?" Mona asks.

"Something like that," I say.

"Awesome! My mom and I thought we should hit the stores up early, just in case we need to order one online or have it cut down or something. Or we might just have one custom made!"

"Yeah, of course. You want it to be perfect," I say. Behind her, Mona's mother is floating around the white dresses, pulling them out, fiddling with the beads, putting them back. She's doing so with such care and affection that it's hard to find it too irritating.

"Do you know what kind of jewelry you're going to wear?" Mona asks, looking over her shoulder at her mom.

"Not a clue. I hadn't really thought about it," I answer.

"My mom wants me to wear these pearls she has — they

were her mother's. But seriously, Shelby, they make me look like an old woman. I want to wear something cute!"

"I'm sure they look fine," I say a little tersely. "Good luck finding a dress. Let me know what you chose?"

"Sure thing," Mona says, and bounds off after her mother.

"Do you suppose they make a medication for whatever it is she's got?" Jonas asks.

"If so, I'd like it in tranquilizer-dart form," I answer as I make my way toward the dressing rooms. This store has only two dressing rooms in the formal-wear department, each with ridiculous circular platforms in the center. Lucky for me, they back up to each other and thus the doors are on opposite sides; if Mona's mother saw the dresses Kaycee was bringing in for me, she'd have a conniption.

"I can't believe *she's* taking a virgin vow seriously," Ruby comments as we reach the dressing room. "She always struck me as the naughty-little-church-girl type, sans the plaid skirt." Ruby and Jonas sink down in chairs just outside the door, Ruby kicking her legs up and over the side. A store clerk gives her a dirty look, which Ruby ignores.

"She's not taking it seriously," I say quietly. "In fact, I'd say I'm the only one who *is*."

"You're only taking it seriously because of the Promises," Jonas says.

"Yeah, but at least I'm taking it seriously," I mutter.

I duck into the dressing room. My gown options are hanging on all the walls. It looks like a chiffon factory threw up in

120

here. I wonder what dresses Mom would have picked out for me. Tasteful, white, classy, I suppose. We'd be here making fun of her own dress's puffy sleeves, or laughing about the *Star Wars* cake story I'd have told her as soon as Dad and I got home. Of course, if she were alive, there'd be no Promises, and I wouldn't care about some vows at a stupid dance. I'd pick out a dress and go through the motions and be perfectly happy about it.

It'd be so much easier.

I slide my sundress off and pull the nearest dress off the rack — a cyan-colored number that fluffs out so far from my body that I could probably smuggle Ruby and Jonas into the ball underneath it. I step out; Ruby's and Jonas's expressions say it all. I go back into the dressing room and give another dress a shot, this one a sort of lavender.

"I look like a cupcake," I mutter as I step outside.

Jonas snorts. I return to the room.

Seventeen dresses later, I'm down to the orange gowns, which I'm pretty sure flatter *any* ethnicity other than alabaster white. Kaycee offers assistance on a few, but considering her advice that "magenta is *the* color for the Crewe family," I'm pretty sure I can't trust a thing she says. The last dress is a bright orange shade that one usually only sees on traffic cones.

Ruby cringes when I step outside. "Holy neons, Batman. Shelby, if you wear that, I will never speak to you again. In fact, I'll light you *and* the dress on fire, then leave and never speak to you again."

"This sucks," I answer, slipping back into the dressing room and slamming the door.

"Don't go away mad. Just go away and change," Jonas says, laughing.

I tear the tangerine gown off my body like it's attacking me and kick it to the side. I can hear Mona giggling through the changing-room wall, then her mother's voice, just like Mona's, only without the bubblicious sound.

Fun, sugary Mona, dress shopping with her mom. It must be nice, having a mom to go dress shopping with. Instead I've got an aunt who wants to dress me like a mojito. What is she going to do if I ever get married? Am I doomed to wear a pineapple on my head, surrounded by fuchsia-clad brides-maids? I would do that to make Mom happy, but my willing-ness doesn't extend to Kaycee.

For a moment, a horrible moment, I'm angry at Mom. I've been angry with her before, of course—for dying, but I've never been angry with her for the Promises. The Prom-ises have always guided me, helped me, but now they're hurt-ing me. They're making me stand in this dressing room, making me vow to Dad, making me participate in this stupid ball, and they're all her fault. She made me promise—she made me promise when she knew I couldn't say no.

I flash back to her in the hospital bed, the papery feeling of her fingers, the desperation in her eyes. She knew she was going to die, I know that now. She knew the end was near, and she didn't tell me. She just made me promise. The Prom-ises were more important than telling me she was dying; the Promises were her good-bye.

I have to keep them. I hate that I have to keep them. I

inhale, swallowing the feeling of dough rising in my throat. I have to keep them.

"Shelby?" Kaycee calls just as I emerge from the dressing room. "Which one did you like?"

"Whatever," I say, walking toward the cash registers. "I'll get whatever one was your favorite."

"Personally," Kaycee says, pausing like a game-show host about to reveal fabulous prizes, "I just adore the pale bluey-green one. What's the color called? Ocean fiesta?"

I don't answer. Kaycee shrugs and throws the dress on the counter, loudly proclaiming that she's a longtime customer and has a frequent-shopper card.

"So, Shelby, I was thinking we could go to a few more stores—I've got a little shopping of my own to do...."

"I have a headache. Can we go home?" I ask bluntly.

"Oh, but Macy's is having a shoe blowout! Just a little longer? Do you want to go wait in the car?" Kaycee asks, eyes widening like I've just kicked her favorite puppy.

"Sure," I mutter. Kaycee makes a *squee* noise that actually *does* give me a small headache and begins talking about stilettos versus wedges with the woman behind the counter. I turn sharply and walk away. Ruby and Jonas are fast on my heels.

"We should scratch 'Ocean fiesta is the shade of whores' in the side of her car," Ruby suggests.

"Sounds good," I mumble over my shoulder, deftly avoiding a pack of women with strollers by slipping through the purse section.

Ruby falls silent; Jonas's turn. In true Jonas fashion, he doesn't speak. Instead, as I weave through the ladies' gloves section, he reaches forward and hooks his arm through mine.

We reach Kaycee's car in silence. I climb into the driver's seat and crank the AC up, waiting anxiously for the warm air in the vents to become icy cool, while Ruby and Jonas sprawl out in the back, doors open so the heat inside the car can escape.

"You know," Jonas finally says, his voice edged with relief as the cold air begins to flow toward the back of the car, "I'm beginning to think your dad is adopted. No way he's related to Kaycee."

"Well," I say, "there's always the possibility that Kaycee was kidnapped and raised by drag queens or exotic dancers."

"No one should love sequins that much." Ruby nods sagely. She scans the parking lot and her face lights up. "Ooh, Shelby, there's a 7-Eleven over there, past that exit ramp! We should go get Slurpees."

"You're suggesting we walk across a five-lane highway for colored corn syrup and ice?" Jonas asks.

"No," Ruby says, "I'm suggesting we *drive*."

I adjust the rearview mirror so I can give Ruby a surprised look.

"Come on, we don't even have to tell Stripperella," Ruby continues. "We'll just go over there real fast and be back before she's out of her shoe coma. It'll take, like, five minutes, tops."

"She'll freak if I drive her car," I say, leaning my seat back.

It's silent for a minute until I hear Jonas squirming. I look back to see him removing his wallet. He pulls the Life List out of the billfold.

"What're you doing?" I ask.

"Check out number one hundred thirty-four."

My eyes run down the list. Number one-thirty-four is written in the margins in old pencil, but I still know what it is.

"Steal a car?" I read it aloud.

"Hey, you're the one who wanted it on the list," Jonas says. "But you could knock that one out this afternoon. I mean, we have a car, we have the keys, and we have a victim who is unlikely to press charges unless we crash into her favorite glitter factory and halt production."

"Plus, she'll be in the mall for ages. I bet we have it back before she ever notices you stole it," Ruby adds.

"Does this even really count as stealing?" I wonder as I run my hands across the car's steering wheel. Everything in it is shiny, like she just got it from the dealership. If I was going to steal a car, this is really the one to take.

"I think so. Come on," Jonas says in an unusually mischievous voice. "Just run up to 7-Eleven and back."

He waggles the Life List in front of me. Promise Three, a life without restraint. If I can have sex to keep the Promises, surely I can take Kaycee's car for a spin.

I bite my lip and shut the driver's side door. Ruby squeals in delight while Jonas clambers over the center console and into the passenger seat. I slide the car into drive and ease forward through an empty parking lot. The next thing I know, I'm on the road that circles the mall, easing along so slowly that cars gun around me every few moments.

"You know, Shelby, you can go a little faster," Jonas suggests.

"Shut up. I'm focusing," I respond, unable to stop the grin that's slowly spreading over my face. 7-Eleven grows closer. Each inch between Kaycee and me makes me feel more at ease.

"Right there," Ruby says, throwing herself across the backseat to point. "Shelby? Right there. The turn is...um... you missed it." She looks longingly at the 7-Eleven as we cruise by.

"I know," I answer. "We're going to the other 7-Eleven."

"What other one? The one by the movie theater?" Jonas asks. I nod, never taking my eyes off the road.

"Um...you realize it'll take, like, an hour to get there and back with traffic," he says.

"Not just traffic," I say. "We've got to stop by the lake, too."

"Oh, man," Jonas groans. "Look, Shelby, I was only encouraging this because I thought you were just zipping up the street. You realize your aunt is going to notice her car is gone if we're gone for *hours*? Have you seen what happens to car thieves? I've played *Grand Theft Auto*, Shel, and the thief always ends up being shot by a cop."

"But they also get to hang out with all those hookers!" Ruby reminds him. Jonas rolls his eyes.

"I promise I'll fight off both the cops *and* the hookers for you, Jonas," I tell him. Jonas shakes his head and releases a small, nervous laugh.

"Fine. But you also have to buy the Slurpees."

"Ooh, good call, Jonas," Ruby says from the backseat. She's considerably more relaxed than Jonas, lying down across the three seats and chewing on her hair.

We cross through the mall area, finally leaving the array of shops and giant inflatable *SALE!* balloons behind us. The main road to the other 7-Eleven is flanked by trees and apartment complexes, with tiny gas stations peppered here and there. We roll down our windows so that the summer breeze mixes with the icy air-conditioning; the blend of the two temperatures makes me ever aware of where we are, what we're doing.

We stop at an intersection and for a moment I don't recognize it—I usually come to it from another direction, so the Citgo and Subway don't appear in their normal spots. If I were to take a left, though, we'd be on the same road that the hearse traveled to my mom's grave. I flash back. White coffin, pink flowers, black dresses, Life List, slide-show music, Dad's tears, and the sudden, awful fear when we walked away from the grave site hours later: We were leaving her there. We were leaving her there, all by herself, under the ground.

She knew she was dying, and she didn't tell me.

"Shelby?" Jonas says. "The light is green."

"Oh," I say. I don't accelerate. Jonas follows my line of sight down the road and seems to get the idea.

"Want me to drive?"

"No." I shake my head. She knew she was dying, and she gave me the Promises. She gave me something to hold on to. I urge the car forward. "No, I'm okay. Sorry."

The stabbing feeling in my heart slowly fades as we continue down the road. The other 7-Eleven is "the crappy one." It's the sort of place where you stop for gas if you absolutely have to but never, under any circumstances, stop to use the bathroom. I park the car far away from the rusty vehicles that occupy most of the lot, and we wade through the heat to get inside.

"Man, this one doesn't have cherry," Ruby gripes, settling for grape.

"But the other one doesn't have blue raspberry," I point out as I slide a giant cup underneath the blue raspberry spout.

"That's not even a real flavor. Have you ever actually seen a blue raspberry? It's just the Slurpee makers' excuse for not being able to come up with a real raspberry flavor."

"You put a lot of thought into this, Ruby," Jonas says as he chooses blue raspberry as well.

"There's not a lot to do on slow days at Flying Biscuit," Ruby says.

I pay for all three Slurpees, and we climb back into Kaycee's car. I drive faster now, more confident with the car's power, and within a few moments we're rumbling down a broken-pavement road toward Lake Jocassee.

This is the side of the lake I prefer; the other half is covered with water parks and rich people's vacation homes, but this side is more subdued. A playground that's faded from sunlight sits near the edge of the water, and in the distance speedboats race by. There's a couple with a little girl having lunch at the picnic table, but other than that, the area is empty. I park the car in a gravel lot, and we get out, Slurpees in tow. The old trestle is visible in the distance—I think I can make out people on its edge.

Ruby and I immediately head for the swings; Jonas sits on the side of a plastic camel on a metal spring. We all rock back and forth gently as the wind stirs the oak trees above. The little girl runs toward us, kicking up wood chips with her pink tennis shoes.

"You look like my pony!" the little girl declares, pointing at Ruby.

The girl's mom is quick to start over, cheeks red-hot.

"What does your pony look like?" Ruby asks.

"His name is Patches!"

"Ah, of course. Pinto," Ruby says with a nod, looking down at her multitone skin. "I guess that's better than a Clydesdale."

The girl's mom reaches the swings. "I'm so sorry, sorry. Come on, Maddie, let's go feed the ducks."

"No, it's okay," Ruby says, holding up her hand. She rises from the swings. "Can I explain it to her?"

The mom doesn't answer for a moment but then shrugs.

"So," Ruby begins as all three start toward the water's edge, "it's this thing called vitiligo that makes me look like Patches, and it doesn't suck as bad as you might think...." she begins. Ruby talks to kids like they're adults; she thinks it makes her bad with anyone under the age of twelve, but I think they appreciate it.

Ruby, Maddie, and Maddie's mom open a bag and start throwing bread to an ever-increasing crowd of ducks, whose flapping wings and quacks eventually drown out Ruby's voice.

I twist the swing in circles, tangling the chain above me. Jonas walks over and takes the swing Ruby was sitting in. He removes his wallet, thumbs through the billfold, and emerges with my Life List. Jonas holds it out for me. I pluck it from his hands, cradling the soft paper in my palm.

I look at item one-thirty-four, then lean down toward Ruby's purse and rummage around for a pen. I hand it to Jonas, who carefully crosses off *Steal a car.*

"One down," he says. "And...four hundred thirty-two to go."

"Four-thirty-two?" I ask, surprised.

"I counted after the trestle jump."

"We should stop adding things," I say, but I know that's not going to happen. Jonas and I have already discussed it before: A life without restraint means an *entire* life. From the time I made the Promise till my last breath.

"Maybe we *should* stop listening to Ruby's additions, though. I noticed all of hers cost upward of five thousand dollars. That weightless thing she was talking about? Six figures."

"Ugh. Add 'get rich' to the list, then," I joke as I twist myself in circles till the swing chain is tight over my head. "So with that, it's four hundred thirty-three."

"We'll get there," Jonas says. "Eventually. I'll be ninety-seven years old holding onto this list."

"Still going to be the keeper of the list at ninety-seven?" I ask, peering through my hair at him. I pull my feet off the ground and the swing begins to unwind rapidly, spinning me around.

"Of course," Jonas says, and sounds offended that I'd suggest otherwise. I try to look at him, but I'm spinning so quick that he's just a blur. "If you'll still be following it," he adds.

"I'll still be following it," I say as the swing comes to a stop. The world still shakes a little; I close my eyes to cure the dizziness. When I open them, I'm looking at Jonas, though he's all blurry. "You're stuck with me, then. Till we're old and Kaycee's giving me Botox gift certificates."

"Kaycee will probably give you Botox gift certificates for graduation. But speaking of the list and Promises and all," Jonas interrupts himself, "you're still planning to go to the wrap party?"

"I am. Ben will be playing the role of the dashing love interest. I'll be the prostitute with a heart of gold," I tease. "Antics will ensue."

Jonas chuckles. "Wait, prostitute? You're getting paid? I get a cut, then, right?" I laugh back, and Jonas sighs before continuing. "The world is thine oyster, Shelby Crewe, that you with sword shall open. Even if that oyster is Ben Simmons, unfortunately."

I open my eyes and shrug.

"*The Merry Wives of Windsor.* It's Falstaff speaking, Shelby, come on!"

It's only an hour before we head back to the mall, sweaty but filled with some sort of joy that only comes from lakeside parks and Slurpee drinking. We leave the windows down so the scent of sunshine and leaves can pour into the car, and I speed up until the outside world is streaming by, like we're in some sort of time machine by ourselves. Just us, no one else, no vows, no death, no ball gowns. I think for a moment that surely this is the best thirty-minute car ride I'll ever experience.

Of course, that's until we see the police cars in the parking lot.

"Oh, shit," Ruby utters. There are two cop cars parked around the spot where Kaycee's car was. Kaycee is standing beside the cops, dozens of shopping bags at her feet.

"We could just turn around," I say nervously as my stomach flips. "I bet we can make it to the South Carolina border before they catch up to us."

"If you run in *Grand Theft Auto*, you typically get shot even faster," Jonas answers. We aren't given much of a choice anyhow. Kaycee suddenly points toward us, practically jumping up and down. Two portly cops turn in our direction and fold their arms over their chests. For a tiny moment, I entertain the notion that Kaycee was worried about me, but then I see the anger on her face. Her eyes scan the car as we pull up, probably checking for dents. I inhale deeply, and the three of us get out.

Kaycee begins to yell, but her words are so shrill that it's hard to tell what she's saying.

"Yes, ma'am, why don't you just stand over here for a moment while we talk to your niece and her friends?" one of the cops says through a bushy mustache. He rolls his eyes at Kaycee as soon as he's turned his back, and he and the other cop — this one a little lankier and younger — step toward us.

"Shelby Crewe, I presume?" the older cop — Officer Woolrow, according to his badge — says.

"Yep," I say through a grimace.

"And," Woolrow looks at a notepad, "Jonas and Rosie?"

"Ruby," Jonas corrects him. Ruby glares at him, as if to say "Way to blow a perfectly good cover." She's so pale that the dark and light facets of her skin contrast more than normal.

Woolrow doesn't seem too bothered by it, though. He sighs and hands the notepad to his partner. "Well, Miss Crewe, did you have permission to take your aunt's car?"

"We...um...had the keys."

"I don't believe that's what I asked," Woolrow says, raising an eyebrow and leaning forward a little. He's remarkably like a guidance counselor; one heartbeat away from saying "What the hell is wrong with you, kid?" but retaining his composure despite it.

"Not exactly," I finally confess. Behind Woolrow, I see my dad's car pulling up.

"Then would you admit that you stole this car for a

joyride?" Woolrow asks. His partner vanishes to both calm Kaycee and talk to my dad, who has just jumped out of his car.

"We didn't mean it!" Ruby bursts, her voice panicky—a tone I didn't know Ruby could take. "Seriously, officer, we just wanted to go to the lake and Jesus Christ Kaycee is crazy-annoying and we really thought we'd have it back before she even knew."

Woolrow nods slowly. "Well, I see what you're saying," he says gruffly, and I wonder if he means the part about Kaycee being crazy-annoying. "Was any damage inflicted upon the vehicle?"

"Nothing," Jonas says. Ruby and I echo him.

Woolrow nods and walks away. Ruby, Jonas, and I cluster together for protection. My dad glances my way, a befuddled look on his face as Woolrow and his partner talk to him. Kaycee joins in, still shouting, then suddenly sways and sits down on the pavement.

"Ma'am, are you okay? Should we call an ambulance?" Woolrow's partner asks as my dad helps her up.

"I'm fine, I'm fine!" Kaycee protests.

"What have you eaten today?" my dad asks, attempting to keep his voice down.

"Exactly what I was supposed to so far...four orange slices and a half cup of brown rice."

"I've got some crackers in the van," Dad says. "Hang on—"

"No! I'm on day four! Day four of the carb-sugar-fat cleanse!" Kaycee says.

Twenty minutes later, Kaycee has eaten one cracker, called the cop fat, and thrown the bag containing my dress at me. But nonetheless, the police informed me she doesn't intend to press charges. Kaycee storms away to her car and peels out of the parking lot, eliciting a few raised eyebrows from the cops. Ruby, Jonas, and I glumly climb into my dad's van.

I wait for his reaction as the cops pull away and my dad starts the engine.

He's silent. I stare at him from the passenger seat. He doesn't look at me, just pulls out of the parking lot and eases the car onto the road we'd been joyriding on a half hour earlier. He drops Ruby off first; she bolts from the car like a freed animal. Then Jonas, who turns to give me a hopeful glance as we pull out of his driveway.

Still silence.

As we pull into our own driveway, my dad finally speaks. "You stole a car."

I pause. Best to play it safe. "Yes," I answer.

"Why?" he asks, and it's a real question. He turns to me, confused, and shuts off the car.

"Because, um..." I think about explaining the Life List, the Promises, *everything*, but I'm not sure he's ready for that. I settle on the sub-reason. "Kaycee is...annoying."

"You stole a car...because my sister is annoying?"

"She..." I sigh and let the words fall from my mouth. "She kept throwing all these candy-colored dresses at me and sweeping around, and I just...I just sort of freaked out." As evidence, I tug the skirt of my ocean fiesta dress from the bag. Even Dad can't help but cringe.

"So when you freak out, you steal your aunt's car?" he asks as I cram Ocean Fiesta back into the bag.

"I guess," I answer meekly. Dad tilts his head, and I'm surprised to see a "could be worse" expression on his face.

"I thought Kaycee would be helpful," Dad says. "You acted like you needed someone to go dress shopping with. Did you not want to go with her?"

"No. I...Kaycee and I are very different," I answer. Read: Kaycee isn't Mom, stop trying to fool me into treating her like she is. The dress bag crinkles in my hands as I twist it up nervously.

"Then why didn't you say something this morning? I would have sent her home," Dad says.

"Because, well...I knew you were trying to help and I felt bad. I didn't want to be mean," I answer. It's true. I did it because of Promise One, but also to avoid the disappointed look that he's giving me right now.

"So you did something you hate just because you didn't want to tell me about it?"

"Something like that."

"But...Shelby, tell me next time. How am I supposed to know?" Dad says. He presses his lips together. "How am I supposed to know anything?"

I get the impression he isn't just talking about Kaycee. I pause for a moment. I could tell him again I don't want to go to the ball. I could tell him how much I hate this.

But then I think that this might be the most in-depth conversation we've had in ages. I think about the cake tasting and how excited my dad was to help me get a dress. How can I reject the ball without his thinking I'm also rejecting him?

Dad watches me; he looks hurt. It makes my heart sink and swell in my stomach. I wish there was something I could say to make it right, but I can't think of anything now that we've all but admitted to the fact that we've been ignoring each other for six years. That we're quietly passing in the night, strangers, two people linked together by a single woman instead of a family of two. And we both know that isn't right, isn't good.

"Anyhow...punishments." Dad pauses and looks at me. He's never really had to punish me before. Thanks, Promise One.

"You could...send me upstairs?" I suggest.

"Okay. Just, uh, go to your room," he says with a sigh, and gets out of the car. I follow, leaving Ocean Fiesta on the floor of the passenger seat.

I've felt a lot of things after keeping the Promises. Joy, relief, closeness to Mom. But this is the first time I've ever felt guilty.

15 days before

Saturday afternoon, Anna comes over to help me get ready—Dad looks a little baffled when she shows up at the door, all highlights and lip gloss, the polar opposite of Ruby and Jonas. It takes four outfits before she gives a jean skirt and tank top the okay—the only thing about my outfit that stays the same are Ruby's naughty panties, which, I'll give her credit, are more comfortable than I had expected.

"You need some jewelry, though. What do you have?" Anna asks. Before I can answer, she's delving into the open box of jewelry on my bathroom counter. She emerges with a pair of purple earrings that I've never worn because they're exceedingly loud and tend to shed glitter onto my shoulders.

"That works," I say, stepping forward to look at myself in the mirror.

"Can I borrow these?" Anna is holding a set of plastic rings that Jonas once bought for me at a cheap costume-jewelry store for Christmas. It was right when I began wearing jewelry more often, so I wore them to prevent him from thinking he'd wasted his money—not because I like them. Anna, however, has a pleading look on her face, like I might not let her out of my house with my precious plastic rings.

"Sure," I say. Anna jumps up and down briefly, grinning. I try to ignore the twang of regret I get when I see Jonas's rings on her fingers.

"Let's go, then! Are you ready for this?" she says, sounding way too much like that sports-game song for my comfort.

"I guess," I say.

Anna drives a much nicer car than Lucinda—something shiny and silver that her parents got her for her birthday. She even has pink windshield-washer fluid. She turns the music up loud and whips the car around corners like a race-car driver. This is the sort of situation that school administrators warn you about, I think.

Ben Simmons lives on the outskirts of town, in a house that sits on a lot of land. That's probably good, because it means his neighbors can't hear the pumping of the bass or shrieks of flirtatious teenage girls that pollute the air when we arrive. The doors are open, letting light flood the front yard. Inside I see half the school dancing or drinking happily. Anna looks at me eagerly, like I should comment on the great work of art before me. I nod and try to look enthusiastic; Anna responds by parallel parking in the worst way, leaving half of her silvery car in the middle of the street. She doesn't fix it—instead, she leaps from the driver's side and beckons me forward, like a girl calling a reluctant puppy.

Anna grabs my hand as soon as I'm within her grasp and practically pulls me to the house. Right before we get to the front door, she drops it, inhales, fixes her hair, and grins excitedly at me.

"Ready?"

"Sure." I guess.

We walk in through the door, and it's sensory overload. Music is pounding, the scent of perfume and sweat and summer and alcohol is heavy in the air, and there are people— so many people—packing into every corner of the house. Their conversations mix together into a steady hum broken apart only by the shouts of guys arguing and giggles of girls hopped up on wine coolers. I scan the room until my eyes land on the party's host.

Ben Simmons is tall and lanky and—weirdly enough— looks a little bit like the gloriously Caucasian Jesus from the church preschool room. He has long hair that he ties back in a low ponytail, bright blue eyes, and chiseled features that you can tell are going to help him hold on to his looks well past his teen years. And he has skin so flawless that if he doesn't use seventeen kinds of skin-care products, then there's no justice in the world. That's right, ladies and gentlemen. I'm about to try to sleep with Jesus from a Proactiv commercial.

"Go talk to him," Anna says.

Suddenly I can't move. I'm not really smitten with Ben Simmons, but that doesn't mean I'm good to march up to him and say, "Mind having a one-night stand with me, Mr. Jesus?" At least with Daniel I felt semi-in-control.

"Take this," Anna says. She grabs two Jell-O shots off a

tray sitting on top of the television and hands them to me. I gulp down both, grimacing as the bite of vodka makes it past the cherry Jell-O flavor. It doesn't make me feel any more confident, despite Anna's encouraging look.

"Here," Anna says. She swallows a Jell-O shot of her own. "I'll help."

She grabs my hand and leads me over to Ben, touching his arm lightly. "Hey, Ben, you remember Shelby—"

"Shelby!" he says. "Wow, haven't talked to you in ages!"

"Hey, I'm gonna go get beers—anyone want any?" Anna asks cheerily. Ben and several guys around him nod and Anna hurries away like a barmaid.

I sit on the edge of a coffee table because there's nowhere else vacant.

"I didn't know you came to parties," Ben says.

"Just not my thing, usually," I say, though I wonder what his definition of *party* is. Apparently it means "party he's at" because I've been to a few smaller get-togethers. Much, much smaller. And much, much less alcohol was involved.

"Cool," Ben says. "So, what kind of stuff are you into these days?"

"Uh, I dance a lot," I say, thinking of my time at Madame Garba's. I don't think one class qualifies as "a lot" but what am I supposed to say? I eat at Flying Biscuit a lot? I'm plotting to lose my virginity? I kind of stole a car?

Ben tilts his head to the side. "Really? You want to dance, then? We have a charming dance floor over by my mom's collection of vintage clown statues."

Shit. Should've seen that coming.

I think I'm way too white to dance to this music. And it's definitely not a waltz.

Say no. Cite some crazy foot injury or something. Pulled a muscle. Had too much to drink. Fear of clown statues. Artificial toes. *Anything. Say no*, my brain repeats.

"Sure!" my mouth says.

I really need to get my brain and mouth on the same page.

What's done is done—Ben tilts his head for me to follow him to the clown-statue dance floor. I try to watch the other girls dancing, both with one another and with mesmerized-looking guys, hoping I can grab a few tips before I'm forced to start. It seems simple—lots of grinding, basically. I've seen enough music videos to get the idea.

Ben puts his hands on my hips like it's nothing, and I fight to ignore the nerves that are leaping up in my chest. We begin to move to the music, and I try hard not to count the beat out loud. Someone passes with another tray of Jell-O shots—I grab one. *Come on, Shelby. You have to do this— you've got to persuade him to sleep with you somehow.*

I'm not as bad as I anticipated. I watch myself as best as possible in the reflection of the TV. I'm not good, by any means—I try to do this move that the cheerleaders seem to have perfected, where they shake their hips and sort of shimmy at once. I abandon that one—it looks more like I'm having a seizure than it does sexy. But that move aside, it's not so bad. Ben doesn't walk away, in the very least, and as the night wears on and I get more brazen, I draw closer to him.

"Want to get out of here?" Ben suddenly leans in and asks me.

Yes. Finally. I don't have it in me to dance another hour. I nod.

Ben takes my hand and leads me upstairs. I catch Anna's eyes briefly, and she grins at me. It's quieter up here; the noise downstairs is muffled and deadened. Ben doesn't turn on the lights, and the sound of our combined breathing becomes louder as we make our way down the hall. When we reach the last door, he grabs a key ring out of his pocket—there's a dead bolt on his bedroom door.

"Pretty intense lock," I say, somewhat drunkenly. I'm at that stage where I don't quite think before I speak, it seems. I'm glad I cut myself off when I did.

"Yeah, I put it on a few years ago, both to keep my parents out and to keep the revelers downstairs from having sex on my bed," he laughs softly. I notice the master bedroom door is wide open.

"So, here we go," Ben says, swinging open the door. His room is small, with a queen-size bed resting unmade in the corner. The walls are covered in theater-performance posters, and the entire room smells a little bit like the drama department's dressing rooms—of cologne and dirty laundry, but not in an entirely unpleasant way.

Ben walks in first. I follow, shutting the door behind me, then clutching my purse to my chest like I'm cold instead of nervous. He sits on the edge of the bed, but I stay standing, pretending to be enthralled by his poster collection.

"So these are, um, all the plays you've been in?" I ask.

"Yep," Ben says, extending a long arm to pull me toward the bed by my jean skirt belt loops. I stagger forward obediently.

"That's a lot of plays," I add. He lifts the corner of my shirt and kisses the side of my stomach. The place tingles, a sensation that spreads around my body in a matter of seconds.

"It is," he murmurs, his breath hot on my skin. He tugs me downward gently, but I tumble onto the bed as if he'd yanked me there.

"I, um..." I begin a sentence, but I have no idea where I'm going with it.

"Come on," he says gently, easily, like he's said it a thousand times before—a confidence that, oddly enough, doesn't dissuade me.

"Okay," I answer breathlessly, dizzy from alcohol and the close scent of his skin. With Daniel, I was the one driving, I was the one leading things. But with Ben, he's in control, a gentle sort of power that I like.

He kisses the side of my stomach again and begins to move up. Remember the Promises, remember the Promises. Ben's hand slides down my side and comes to rest on my hip. He moves it up again, this time reaching under my shirt.

Come on, Shelby. Do this, I tell myself in a voice that sounds a lot like Ruby's. I grab the edge of my shirt and yank it over my head. Ben's eyes widen and a schoolboy-type grin spreads across his face.

"Shelby..." he says almost accusingly. "God, if I'd only known—" And then he eagerly grabs for the buttons on my skirt.

God, if he'd only known. Seems appropriate that a guy who looks like Jesus would reference God while trying to undress a girl. Or maybe horribly inappropriate. I need to remember to tell Jonas about the Jesus comparison; it'll crack him up.

"Here," I say, and swing down to where I dropped my purse on the floor. I dig through it quickly, before emerging with a "strawberry sensations" condom. I kiss Ben and press it into his hand.

"A condom?" Ben asks. I nod and move to kiss him again. He backs up. "Aren't you on birth control or something?"

"Um...no."

"Oh. Most girls are these days. Well, when was your last period?"

Let me log it away that there is nothing—nothing—more unsexy than talking about your bleeding vagina. Seriously— *nothing* more unsexy. The warm, dizzy sensation is swept away and replaced by the realization that his room is a bit chilly.

"A few weeks ago?" I say hesitantly; my face heats up in embarrassment.

"Then we don't have to use a condom anyway," Ben says, a grin replacing the concerned look on his face. He pulls me closer, but the heat of his body isn't warming; it's invasive. Ben tosses the condom over me onto the floor.

"Wait, uh—" I don't get to answer, as his lips are on mine again. They're persuasive, convincing, and I don't protest when he slides a hand down the front of my underwear. But then he presses toward me, and I feel the erection under his pants. I snap out of the lull.

"You have to wear a condom," I say, thinking of the LOVIN rules and my own desire to not have to explain to Dad how I got pregnant.

"I don't like condoms," Ben says, his voice a little irritated. "Trust me, it's better without them."

"No," I answer, this time firmly. I focus on the words *must wear condoms* on Jonas's list, like they'll give me power. "Seriously, I'm not on birth control and I just don't want to risk it." Fear of pregnancy seems kinder than saying "Who knows what I could catch from you."

"Okay, okay, how about this—I'll pull out beforehand."

Um. Ew.

"Come on," I plead, trying to sound sexy or desirable or anything but frustrated. "Just wear it, and we can have sex. It'll be great."

"I hate condoms."

We stare at each other, and suddenly the passion filters away. I don't feel warm and dizzy; I feel annoyed and irritated. Ben contracts away from me so we're barely touching. I stand up so quickly that my vision blacks out for a second, then grab my shirt. I ignore the burning of tears in the corners of my eyes.

"Where are you going?" Ben asks as I begin trying to negotiate my skirt back up my legs.

"I'm leaving," I huff, leaving off the bit "before I cry, you jackass."

"Come on, Shelby," he says. "We can just kiss or do other things. We don't have to have sex."

"All I wanted to begin with was to have sex," I snap back. Ben looks taken aback, both delighted and confused by a girl saying that to him. I don't give him any clarity, though, and I grab my purse as I work an arm through the strap of my tank top. Something is welling up inside me, something angry and hurt and bitter. Before Ben can say anything else, I fling open the door to his bedroom and make my way down the hall.

There's a bathroom at the far end. I swing into it and lock the door. A coconut-scented jar candle is burning, and it provides all the light I need. I sit on the edge of the bathtub and stare at the blue and violet seashells that adorn the shower curtain.

Guy number two, failed. At least this one wanted to have sex with me, I try to tell myself, but a deep feeling of failure is rising through my chest and into my throat. A choked sob emerges but doesn't become full-fledged tears. I'm still willing to have sex, but still unable. I suck.

Dumbass Jesus look-alike. Just as disappointing as the one painted in the church classroom. No wonder I like the historical Jesus Jonas described to me better—dark hair, dark eyes, bearded, more Persian than Caucasian. I wonder if he ever tried to have sex. Was he human enough for that? You're not supposed to think about that, I guess, the same way you aren't supposed to think about your parents having sex.

How is it possible that God understands what's best for me, what I should or shouldn't do, if he isn't human? If he hasn't loved someone, hasn't lost someone, hasn't wanted someone? Why did I reach out for him when the world crumbled, out for the hand of some being who doesn't know what it's like to lose a mother?

Because I was told he'd have the answers. I was told he was what I needed, when what I really needed was Mom. What I really needed was a person, a real person, not an invisible being, who could show me that everything would be okay again, that I wouldn't spend the rest of my life crying. A person like Mom.

A person like Dad, I think. I've always thought Mom was the only one keeping the ground from crumbling, but maybe Dad was part of the glue holding it together, too. Maybe he needed someone to grab onto as badly as I did.

A sharp rap at the door scatters my thoughts.

"Shelby? It's Anna! Are you okay? Open the door!"

I inhale the scent of coconut, trying to clear the misery from my head. I rise and open the door. Anna prances in, slams the door behind her, and locks it. She lowers the toilet lid and sits down, crossing her legs and leaning forward, first with enthusiasm, then concern when she sees my face.

"What happened? Are you okay? You look upset," Anna says, and her eyes are so genuine that it almost takes me by surprise.

"Nothing happened," I say with a shrug. "I'm not upset. I mean, I am, but...never mind. Nothing happened."

"Because if he did anything, you tell me, Shelby. I can start a rumor about him having crabs or something. I'm great at rumors," she says, looking proud.

I laugh but shake my head. "It's okay. Really. I wanted to have sex with him, but he wouldn't wear a condom, so I said no."

Anna nods. "Naturally. Ugh, I hate it when guys are like that. I don't get what the big deal is about condoms."

"Me neither," I say. "Especially when I was practically throwing myself at him. I mean, it's just a condom!"

"I got lucky," Anna says. "First time I had sex, it wasn't an issue at all. I mean, he actually had condoms. I didn't need to bring them. They were even the 'for her pleasure' type."

I raise an eyebrow—it's not exactly surprising news to hear Anna isn't a virgin, but it's still a tidbit I didn't know. "Who was it with?" I ask.

Anna frowns at me, uncrosses her legs, and sits back. "I...oh."

"What?"

"I just thought...I dunno, I thought you knew."

"No," I answer, sighing and trying to hide my irritation that Anna thinks everyone else keeps hookup charts with the intensity she does.

Anna bites her lip, squirms, then speaks. "Sorry, Shelby.

I really thought he'd have told you. I mean, God, he tells you everything."

Wait. Something in my stomach tightens. My head feels hot and my throat thick.

"Who was it, Anna?" I ask.

Anna shrugs and picks at the toilet seat cover for so long that I want to scream. *Just say it, Anna. Say it.*

"Jonas."

14 days before

A clock in the hallway chimes midnight. I listen to it through the wall, trying to focus on the tinny sound of fake bells so I don't have to think about what Anna just said. And I don't have to think about why it makes me feel this way. So...

Hurt.

It hurts—it hurts everywhere. My brain tries to reason with me, reminds me that Jonas isn't mine. We've never dated, never been together, never even suggested it to each other. But every fiber of me shouts something different— that Jonas *is* mine, somehow, in some strange way. Some way that means it isn't okay that Anna slept with him, and it's even less okay that he didn't tell me. Something is burning in my chest, slowly eating away at me, something I can't name.

"Shelby?" Anna says meekly.

"Huh? I..." I grasp for words.

"Sorry. Is that okay? I mean, that I slept with him?"

"Um...I just didn't know. I didn't know he'd had sex at all," I mumble.

"He hadn't before me," she says. "It was just this thing. It was last year. We were hanging out after school while you were hanging out with some other guy, Danny or David or Daniel or something. And then he offered to give me a ride home and...I don't know. I mean, I think he's cute. And it just kind of happened."

"I don't understand—were you dating?" I ask, words finally coming a little easier. Now that the shock is passing, my mind is flooded with questions, things I don't want to know but *have* to know at the same time.

"No." Anna shrugs. "We talked about it. I mean, we'd been hanging out a little more often since you were with Daniel."

Why did he keep it from me that long? Why didn't I realize it on my own? Did he know I'd be mad?

Surely not. I didn't even realize something like this would make me so mad.

"So just...just the once?"

"Yeah," she says. "I didn't think it was that big of a deal, but he acted like it was. And then you and Daniel broke up, and he and I kinda stopped hanging out, for the most part." She pauses, watching me carefully. When I take too long to sort the tangle of words in my head, she speaks again. "I didn't think it was that big a deal, Shelby."

"It...it isn't," I say, shaking my head. "It totally isn't. We aren't together." I'm lying, I can tell, but I'm not sure about what.

"Yeah, that's what I figured. I mean, I wouldn't have done it if you were," she says.

"Yeah..." We aren't together, why does it matter if he

slept with someone? How is it any of my business who Jonas is in bed with? It's not. It shouldn't matter.

But then, why does it matter so, so much?

"I need to go," I finally say. "I need to leave."

"You sure?" Anna says with a small pout.

"Yes," I say firmly. "I just... I need to go home."

"I'll take you. Let me go find my purse."

I slide into Anna's car, trying not to think about her and Jonas. About her naked, about *him* naked, about them kissing, together, touching in ways I can't understand. She didn't think it was a big deal—did that bother him? Why didn't he talk to me? Why didn't he tell me? I'm not sure what's making me feel so betrayed—the sex or the secrets.

"Hey, Shelby?" Anna calls out twenty minutes later as I step out of her car into my darkened driveway. It's the first we've spoken since leaving the party—I was too preoccupied with thoughts of Jonas to break the awkward silence that hung over the car.

"Yeah?" I answer faintly.

"Sorry things didn't work out with Ben. There are more fish in the sea," she says optimistically.

"Sure," I answer, and turn to trudge away without saying good-bye. I hear Anna's car backing out of the driveway and squealing down the street.

That's right. Things didn't work out with Ben. I'd almost forgotten—my head doesn't have room for failed sex and the news that my best friend slept with Anna Clemens. My head doesn't have room for anything else. I slip inside and hurry upstairs to my bedroom.

Relax. Calm down, Shelby.

What do I do? Do I call Jonas? Yell at him? Ask him to tell me the truth? Should I mention it at all? Should I forget it and focus on the LOVIN plan?

What do I do, Mom?

I squeeze my eyes shut and picture Mom the same way I always do, us in her bedroom, me lying across the bed while she casually folds laundry. *Talk to me. Tell me what to do.*

Mom smiles and pauses at pairing socks to stroke my hair, but she doesn't answer.

And so I recite the Promises to myself, because they're the only thing I know for certain anymore.

13 days before

The next day, the heavy feeling in my stomach dissipates into quiet anger. I've been avoiding Jonas—he's called seven times, but I sent them to voice mail, and when I talk to Ruby, I hurry her off the phone. How can I talk to either of them about anything but the fact that Jonas slept with Anna Clemens? How am I supposed to explain why it bothers me when even I don't understand?

Dad is sitting at the dining room table when I clunk down the stairs in my pajamas. "We have to make goodie bags. The lady who was supposed to won a trip to Cabo off the radio and doesn't have time to do them," he says upon seeing me. He rubs his temples and yawns.

"Goodie bags? Is the cake and dress and ball not enough of a prize?" I ask.

I'm almost surprised to be reminded of the ball—Jonas and Anna have taken the priority position in my head to the point where I can't focus on much else.

"It won't be so bad," Dad says, a poor attempt at cheerfulness. "There's a catalog with all sorts of Princess Ball stuff in it. We can just pick it out and put it in bags. We'll have to get it rush-shipped, though...."

I sigh and sit down at the other end of the table. "All right." Dad slides the catalog across the table to me.

"And..." he begins again.

"Not more," I groan.

"We have to come up with a symbolic activity. Something that shows the, um...bond...between the fathers and daughters."

"A what?"

"It's different every year. Like, at some balls, the father and daughter actually exchange rings," he says, coughing a bit. I flinch, so he tries another route. "There's also a thing where the fathers stand on either side of an aisle holding up swords, and you put down a white rose—"

I blink. "Swords?"

"Awfully medieval, isn't it? I'm not sure programmers are supposed to even touch swords," my dad says, and I laugh a little, then pause.

"What did Mom do at hers?"

Dad inhales and looks down. "If I remember correctly, I think she said they all read a poem or excerpt aloud. Something they thought symbolized their relationship with their father. We joked around about it all spring, our friends, because your mom said she was going to read something from a romance novel as a joke."

"Did she?"

Dad laughs a little. "No, because she was afraid they

wouldn't realize it was a joke, and her father would get arrested. I don't think she ever really planned on doing it."

"What did she read from, then?"

He thinks for a moment. "*To Kill a Mockingbird*. But I don't remember which passage."

I try to remember the book, try to channel my mom and figure out which line she would have chosen, but all I can remember is failing the test on it in ninth grade. It makes me feel guilty, makes my stomach twinge.

"What if we did that, then? The readings?" I say.

"Sounds good. Well, then. After we make the goodie bags, I confirm the cake order, and we go to that second dance lesson, I'd say we're finished, Shelby. Except the questionnaire—we're supposed to go over those...."

"Right...yes." My questionnaire isn't entirely complete—to be honest, I've hardly thought about it lately.

"Is..." Dad looks at his hands, takes a long swig of orange juice. "Is everything okay? We don't have to share the questionnaires if you don't want to...."

My eyes widen a bit in surprise—well spotted, Dad. I'm not sure he's ever been that tapped in to my mood before. I open my mouth, try to find a way to explain without *actually* explaining. I'm not horrified by the idea of talking to Dad anymore, but that doesn't mean I'm ready to spill all the details of Jonas and Anna, much less how I found out about them. "It's not the questionnaires. Just some stuff with Jonas," I finally say.

"Like what?" Dad asks, and his voice is so real, so curious, that I can't imagine not answering.

"I found out he was dating this girl from school and didn't tell me." When I say it like that, it sounds so stupid. I half expect Dad to laugh or shrug it off.

"Oh," Dad says instead, nodding seriously. "Have you asked him about it?"

"No," I say. "I've been avoiding it, really."

Dad frowns. "You can't just hold that in. You've gotta be honest with the people you love."

Wow. *Love.* The word leaves his mouth so easily that I inhale, unsure what it means. Does he think I'm in love with Jonas? Is that why I feel so betrayed? *Am* I in love with him and just didn't realize it?

Whoa. I guess deep down, I must have known that was a possibility — why else would Anna's news bother me so much? But thinking it so directly makes it different, makes it possible. Makes me think it might be true.

"You think I love Jonas?" I ask Dad faintly.

Dad raises his eyebrows, surprised. "I mean, he's your best friend. I assume you love your best friend."

"Oh." Platonic love, that's what he meant. "Right. Of course I love him." There's never been any doubt that I love Jonas in that regard. Though now I can't shake the wonder: Are my feelings stronger than even *I* thought?

"That's my advice — for what it's worth, anyway," Dad says. "Your mom had to tell me the truth about how she felt. I'd never have believed she could love me if I hadn't heard it from her."

I manage a small laugh as Dad rises and gives me a short

clap on the shoulder. Would Mom's advice have been the same? Does it matter? Guilt overpowers the anger at Jonas for just a moment: Dad is here. Dad is giving me advice from the heart. And here I am, trying to talk to Mom, who isn't here, instead of Dad, who is.

But that doesn't mean I'm ready to talk to Jonas. I want to wait, wait till I know I won't yell, wait till I know I understand what our relationship is. Because right now? I don't understand anything.

Maybe I never did.

12 days before

"I'm supposed to pick out stuff for goodie bags," I say, dropping the heavy catalog onto a wet spot on the well-worn table.

Ruby ignores the cook calling her order up, balancing a tray of orange juices like some sort of diner circus performer. She peers over my shoulder at the catalog's table of contents.

"They sell accessories for these things? Jesus Christ."

"Exactly—necklaces with Jesus Christ on them are apparently a bestseller for this sort of thing. But then there's also weird stuff, like...I dunno, cake tins. Princess Ball–themed cake tins."

"Cake tins, huh?" Ruby says, green eyes sparkling mischievously. She sets her tray of drinks down on my table. "Dare I ask what they're in the shape of?"

"Castles," I reply, flipping to a page full of silver castle-shaped tins. "And hearts."

Ruby giggles. "I've got a few cake tins from my sister's bachelorette party that would be more fitting for a virgin fest. What'd you pick out?"

I turn to a dog-eared page in the back of the catalog.

"Among other things, this." I point to a page full of bright red shirts that say things like *Always a Princess* and *Her Royal Highness* and, my favorite, the one I'm pointing to, which proclaims, *I'm waiting for my prince.*

"Oh, my," Ruby says. "I see what you did there, Princess Ball. Clothes for the proudly celibate. Which style?"

"I'm thinking I'll go with the 'fitted baby rib' cutout tee." I snicker. Ruby laughs loudly, causing a few diners to raise their eyebrows in our direction.

"Perfect," she answers, tapping the huge-boobed blond model wearing the "fitted baby rib" style. The words are stretched across her chest in a way that definitely contradicts the cursive message. "But let me know if you want those cake tins, Shelby. You know, just to show the supposed virgins what bits of the male anatomy to avoid."

"Will do. I brought Ocean Fiesta, by the way, if the offer for you to turn it into something less...um...'frothy' is still available."

"Of course it is. I would never turn down the opportunity to work miracles," Ruby says, eyes gleaming. "But you can't be mad at me if I rip some of those sequins off."

"Please. Donate them to Kaycee's Sequins for the Poor cause."

"Seriously?" Ruby asks, her eyes wide.

I laugh. "No, but would you be surprised if I told you she ran a charity about sequins?"

"Not really. By the way, I still haven't heard how things went with Ben! Jonas said he hasn't heard how it went, either—you should seriously call him, by the way. He's getting worried about you. Anyway, still got your chastity in check?"

I swallow the urge to ask Ruby if she knew about Jonas and Anna. "Wouldn't wear a condom. I know that health classes sort of go above and beyond to scare the hell out of people about having sex, but even *I* understood the whole 'condom is a must' rule."

Ruby nods. "Maybe Ben thinks condoms are just another scare tactic. You know, 'Oh, God, if you have sex you have to seal your organs in rubber and it's awful' instead of 'It feels the same and you don't get the Herp.' Not that you have the Herp, Shelby, just saying."

"Right," I say, smiling.

"So you're on to the next guy on the list?"

Right. Guy number three. I nod.

"Who is he?"

I grimace. "I don't have one, actually. No one came to mind, and I sort of figured that between Daniel and Ben, something would happen."

"I've got somebody for you, remember?" Ruby says mysteriously. She points across the restaurant at Jeffery, the guy she mentioned right after school let out. "Jeffery asked me if you were single a few weeks ago."

"I don't want to date him, though," I say.

"Yeah, but...desperate times call for desperate measures? And who knows, Shelby. Maybe you'll end up in love with him."

"Maybe," I say, but I don't believe it. "Should I talk to him?"

"I'll let him know you're interested. And I'll imply what you're interested in so there's no issue, okay?"

"Sounds good," I say slowly, watching Jeffery from across the diner. He's an attractive guy—dark hair, dark eyes, the kind of guy who might play in an indie band and ride his bike to work. He's a stranger, though, and something about that renews my worry about the LOVIN plan. Can I go through with losing my virginity to a total stranger?

"Why don't you talk to Jonas and see what he thinks about Jeffery?" Ruby suggests at my pause.

An image of Jonas and Anna together flashes through my head. "No," I tell Ruby quickly. "No, it's fine. Talk to Jeffery for me? Maybe we could get together sometime this Saturday?"

"Saturday?" Ruby pouts. "But that's the day the Ridgebrook cheerleaders start summer practice. I wanted you to come with me so we could watch them fall out of the pyramids."

Before I can respond, Ruby grabs her tray of juices and scoots off to see to another table. I circle things from the catalog. *Focus, don't think about Jeffery, don't think about Jonas.* There's a whole page of silk flowers—I circle the red rose, because there's something wrongly sexy about red roses. If I have my way, these will be the most ironic goodie bags ever created.

I sigh and sit back. I'm making goodie bags for a ball I

hate. How lame is that? My thoughts flicker back to my Life List, how it's languishing in the billfold of Jonas's wallet. Somewhere on it is *Put flowers on every grave in a cemetery.* I don't know where it is without Jonas here to show me.

I circle the red silk roses again.

I shouldn't be so lost without Jonas. I could complete my Life List without him, if I had to. I close the catalog and rise. Ruby catches my eye from near the order-up window.

"See you later," I mouth. Because when you have these moments of inspiration, you sort of have to act on them immediately.

*   *   *   *

"I need, um … carnations," I say as I sort through my wallet. I'd like to say roses, but at two dollars apiece I'm pretty sure they'd end up being more than my dad's credit card limit.

"How many and what color?" the girl behind the counter of the flower shop says. I do a double take—it's Christine Juste, one of Anna's friends. She has long hair that was once pink but has now faded, a nose ring, and dirt smudges on both cheeks. Somehow the dirt smudges made her almost unrecognizable to me.

"Christine," I say suddenly, blushing at not realizing it's her sooner.

"Hey, Shelby," Christine says, smiling. "How's your summer?"

"So far it's decent," I say. "Better than school."

Christine nods. "So, you said carnations? How many?"

"How many do you have?"

Christine's eyes widen a little. "We have...fifty or so pink ones, and about two hundred or so white ones. We use whites in bouquets more often," she explains.

"I need about...um..." I do some quick math in my head, thinking about the cemetery layout. "Probably about seven hundred."

Christine pauses. "Is this for that Princess Ball thing?"

"Oh. Yeah. For the ball," I say, feeling stupid I didn't think of that.

"Cool," Christine says, nodding. "I think the idea of it is awesome."

"The idea of Princess Balls?" I ask. Christine never struck me as the Princess Ball type.

"Yeah," Christine says, and laughs a little. "I mean, maybe not the dance part—not really my style. But I like that girls and their dads have something to do together. My dad and I are really close, and it doesn't seem like that's the case with most girls, that's all."

"Right." What am I supposed to say? I agree? I never thought of that? That I can't believe Christine Juste is a better candidate for the Princess Ball pamphlet than Mona Banks? I don't know why I'm so surprised that people aren't always how they seem—after all, I probably don't look like someone questing for a hookup. I nod and make a noncommittal noise.

"Anyway—carnations. Let me see what we have," Christine says, and disappears in a flutter of faded pink hair.

I get lucky and the truck that delivers carnations arrives within a half hour—but that still gets me up to only three hundred. The flower shop employees run around with a sort of giddy gleam in their eyes, collecting daisies and tulips, their second-least-expensive flowers. I make it to seven hundred—but just barely. The total comes to over five hundred dollars. I see Christine's manager grimace a little when I explain that it's my dad's card, but I think that she's so eager to do big business that they swipe the Visa anyhow.

They load the flowers into cardboard boxes and help me shove them into the back of the van, and I set out toward the cemetery. Something has come over me, like the scent of the flowers is intoxicating me and I can't think straight—but it's wonderful. I feel powerful, amazing even, a sort of high I've never gotten from marking off a Life List item before. I've never crossed off a list item without Jonas; I consider calling him, but there's this underlying buzzing in my chest that hums, No. *This is for you to do alone.*

So I go on, by myself.

The intersection is recognizable from this direction, and while memories of Mom's funeral flash by in my mind, they're in the background, afterthoughts of the summer day.

I park the car in the wraparound drive, just beside a giant statue of Jesus. He stands with his arms outstretched, welcoming everyone. Now that I think of it, Ben Simmons doesn't look so much like Jesus after all. I open the back door and throw the lid off the first box, then grab as many flowers as I can manage.

I step up to the first row of graves, all topped with a brass or silver plaque instead of a headstone. The sun makes them sparkly, some almost blindingly so.

Henry Waxman, born 1958, died 2001. I drop a carnation over his name.

Joycelyn Elders, born 1918, died 2004. A daisy.

Arthur Caplan, born 1932, died 2008. Another carnation, a white one. I continue along the row, reading each name before dropping a flower on the nameplate. I manage to circle the Jesus statue three times before I run out of flowers and have to go back to the car.

The names begin to run together in my head, but not in a forgettable way; more like they're joining forces, encouraging me to keep going even though my arm is tired from holding so many flowers. The sun overhead seems to pulse heat down onto my shoulders, and I can feel the deep burn of them starting to turn red. I ignore it and go back to the car again. The spot, the place where my mom lies, is at the other end of the cemetery; I avoid looking at it. I've hardly ever been here without Jonas. *Focus, Shelby.*

Late afternoon, and the sun begins to hide behind the thick oak trees that dot the cemetery. It casts dappled shadows across the ground and I'm running low on flowers. I glance up and see *the* spot as I head back to the car. Only tulips are left, the most expensive of the flowers. The back corner of the cemetery is quiet, the noise from the road almost completely silenced. The sounds of cicadas and birds emerge from the woods on the other side of the cemetery's glossy iron fence. A tulip for Daniel Savage, one for Karola Siegel.

I grab the last bundle of flowers as sunset truly hits the graveyard. The world is dark purple rimmed in gold, and the little light that remains reflects off the headstones in a way that makes them look like ripples on water. Her spot is getting closer—it's unavoidable. But I'm afraid if I stop to look at it, I won't have the courage to start again and finish the job. I drop three more tulips.

She's only four stones away.

Another, and another. I recognize the name of the woman on Mom's left side, Maggie Sanger. I remember wondering what she was like, since she got to be so close to my mom for all eternity. I look down and realize there's only one flower left in my hand; a single pink tulip that's already wilting a bit in the humidity.

I take a step over, to the grave beside Maggie Sanger.

JENNIFER L. CREWE
MARCH 15, 1969-AUGUST 1, 2003
ALWAYS LOVING, ALWAYS LOVED

I always wondered who picked out the line about love but never asked. I stare at the stone, trying not to think about the white coffin beneath it. I bend down and run my fingertips over the image of a lily that rests above the *love* line. I brush the tulip bloom across her name.

I used to have this movie idea of death, before Mom died. All you ever really see is the shiny headstones, the beautiful services, the black horses pulling caissons up the road to the cemetery. Bagpipers, priests, dresses—ceremony. But the truth is, when someone dies, you keep thinking of everything else. Once we all left and the funeral home took the blue tent down, I worried that she was cold.

Surely under all that dirt, it has to be freezing? I remember the first winter after she died, the first truly cold day when the ground frosted, how I wanted, more than anything in the world, to be able to put a blanket around her shoulders. I want to help her; I want to be there for her.

I drop to my knees between Mom and Maggie Sanger's grave, and put my hand over the spot where I think Mom's hand might be. My shoulders are sunburned and the grass is sticky. The air is full of the sort of heat that wraps around me, embraces me. It's not cold today—not here, not under the ground. Not in the heaven that I have to believe my mother is in.

That's the real problem I have with God. When the world crumbled, I couldn't grab onto him. But I can't bring myself to deny him completely, because if I do, where does that leave Mom? In heaven alone? In heaven with him despite me? Alone in the ground?

No. I can't think that.

There will always be a part of me that can't abandon the idea of God, because if I do, I have to abandon Mom. No matter how angry I am with him, no matter how much I doubt he is what the church claims, I have to think he's there. I have to think he runs a paradise in the clouds. I have to think Mom is with him. Happy.

I reach over and drop the last tulip on Maggie Sanger's grave, then run my hand across Mom's headstone. I lean over and kiss the word *loved*. *Put a flower on every grave in a cemetery* — if I had to be one flower short, Mom would want to be the one to go without. *Always loving.*

The warm air holds me close even as I walk away.

9 days before

It looks like St. Valentine vomited in my living room.

I am surrounded by boxes overflowing with pink, white, and red trinkets. Goodie bag paraphernalia. I sigh and cram another *I'm waiting for my prince* shirt into a pink canvas bag. I've been at it for two hours and have finished only four bags—I'm not sure if it's because it's an arduous task or because it's a boring one. My mind wanders. I wonder what would happen if I slipped condoms into a few bags? I could even get the strawberry-flavored ones so they match....

Ugh. I toss a heart-shaped candle in on top of the shirt.

I thought about calling Jonas to help—it's a thought that keeps popping up in my head like one of those little Whac-a-Mole games. It pops up; I remind myself that he slept with Anna Clemens and smash it back down.

And then it pops up again. I suck at this game.

Truth is, I know I can't delay calling him much longer. I already had Dad answer my phone and tell him I'm sick, but if I keep this up, Jonas is probably going to show up at my front door. I have to face him sooner or later. I take a deep breath. Just call him.

I grab my phone and dial, fast, before I can change my mind.

"Finally! I was worried," he says when he answers, exhaling in relief. "Why didn't you call? I had to find out from Anna about Ben."

Her name in his voice bites at me. Did she tell Jonas that I know about them? Surely not—I'd be able to tell, wouldn't I? Or does he think it wasn't that big a deal, either?

I hope that's not it.

"Sorry," I say. "I was upset." A half truth, but a truth. "Can you come over? I need help with some ball stuff. I've got to put a bunch of goodie bags together."

"Of course," Jonas says, and I hear him grab his keys. "Be there in ten minutes."

Jonas actually arrives *eleven* minutes later—I know, because I counted them down nervously.

"Hi," I say when I open the door. Jonas smiles, steps in, and hugs me, his arms wrapped tightly around my shoulders. My face involuntarily breaks into a smile, and I return the embrace. It's different, though, not the way he and I normally hug. Is it him, or me? The weight of knowing he slept with Anna is amazingly not as heavy as the question of how I actually feel about him, if I actually love him. I hold on a moment longer than normal, hoping something in his arms will answer my uncertainties.

"Thanks for coming to help," I say when he releases me.

"Glad to help and watch your cable," Jonas says. "I also

had to hear from Ruby that you crossed off a list item without me. Flowers on every grave?"

I blush. "Almost. I was one short, so I didn't put one on my mom's."

He shrugs but looks strangely proud of me. "We'll drop one off sometime, so you can cross it off officially."

I lead him into the living room, where the television is barely visible among the piles of boxes.

Jonas gasps.

"We had to get everything rush-shipped," I explain as Jonas stares at the dozens of boxes with a look of horror on his face.

"Christ, Shelby, since when are goodie bags more than some candy and pencils?"

"Since they became Princess Ball–themed, I'd wager. So, just put one of each item into the bags.... Which box is the bags?" I murmur to myself as I kick the boxes over to read the shipping labels. "Ah, this one. Anyway, just one of each item into the bag."

"Right," Jonas says. He flips on the television to *Animal Cops* and rips the tape off a box of "fresh n' clean"–scented perfume. I think it smells more like pipe cleaner than the lilies and clouds on the box, but whatever.

"There's something really sick about candy in the shape of a cross," Jonas says, holding up one of the white chocolate crosses—they were made special, with the church's name molded onto them. His eyes are dark brown—I mean, they've always been dark brown, but suddenly all I can think about is how different they are from Daniel's or Ben's. And maybe Jeffery's. Can't forget about Jeffery—I wonder what color his eyes are. I look down.

"I know," I say, my voice a little stilted. *Jeffery, think about Jeffery.* I inhale and force words from my lips. "So... since Ben didn't work out, I'm on to guy number three, I guess." I smash a few silk flowers into a bag.

Jonas frowns. "Any idea who?"

"There's a guy who works with Ruby. His name is Jeffery. She said he was interested in me."

"Are you *sure* you want to sleep with a total stranger, Shel?" he asks, raising his eyes to mine.

"I have to. You know that," I say calmly. Jonas's eyes waver. It gives me some sort of sick satisfaction to know the LOVIN plan still bothers him.

"Yeah..." Jonas drifts off and fills the silence that follows by crinkling the cellophane bag of princess-themed rubber bracelets.

I sigh. This isn't what I want—isn't what I need, to irritate, even hurt, my best friend. I need to do what my dad said. I need to talk to him. There's a tiny part of me that, stupid as it sounds, feels like if I never hear *Jonas* admit to sleeping with Anna, it won't be true. But I can't just stay silent.

"I..." I don't know what to say. Jonas looks at me, waiting for me to go on.

"You...?" he says when I can't find the words.

"Anna," I finally spit out. "Anna said something to me at the party."

"About?" he asks.

"You."

They slept together. I mean, I already knew, but the look on Jonas's face confirms it. His eyebrows sink, lips part, breath shortens, like he's afraid to speak. He finally looks back down at his goodie bag and licks his lips.

"You slept with her and didn't tell me?" I ask, though I didn't mean to. The question found its way out of my mouth on its own. I try to smile, make the question light, but the resulting expression is forced and awkward. I look down.

"Shel, I..."

"Why didn't you tell me?" I ask quietly.

"I didn't even mean for it to happen," Jonas explains. "You were with Daniel and I was just...lonely, I guess? And she wanted to and then it just...it just happened. I'm sorry."

"But why didn't you tell me?" I repeat, and any attempt at lightness in my voice is gone.

Jonas inhales and shakes his head, meets my eyes across the room. "I was afraid you'd be mad at me." I don't say anything, so he continues. "And by the looks of it, I was right."

"I'm not mad," I lie. "I mean, I'm not mad you slept with her. I'm mad you kept it from me."

"You're not mad I slept with Anna?" Jonas asks doubtfully.

"No," I say, a little shriller than I intended. "Why should I be?"

"Because…" he begins, but he can't figure out what to say. He tosses a shirt into the bag and then pushes it away from him.

"I don't care," I say. "It doesn't matter to me that you slept with her. Just don't keep secrets from me. But seriously, fuck whoever you want."

"Shelby," Jonas says, confusion in his tone. "You don't mean that."

"Why wouldn't I?" I ask. "We aren't together, Jonas. You're allowed to have sex with whoever you want. I mean, you aren't mad I'm going to have sex with Jeffery, are you?"

There's a long silence. Jonas finally sighs and shakes his head. "No. You have to do it to keep the Promises. It's fine," he says shortly.

Why was that not the answer I wanted to hear?

The conversation ends there, and the room fills with the sounds of the TV and the slow, irritating cadence of bags being filled. There's more I want to say, but I'm not sure exactly what it is. Whatever it is, it's eating at me from the inside out. I bite my lips and cram a pair of pink nail polishes into a bag.

Jonas sighs and sits back, then meets my eyes for a long time. "Do you want me to go?" he asks slowly.

"Why?"

"Because I…" he looks at me meaningfully. But I don't move, don't blink, don't look away. He presses his lips together, and when they part he speaks fast. "I lied. I don't want you to sleep with Jeffery. And I don't want you to go

176

through with the LOVIN plan. I think you're taking the Promises too far."

"You know I have to keep them," I snap.

"Not like this," Jonas says.

"Why do you care?" I ask slowly. "Why does it matter to you if I get laid?"

There's a flicker in the back of my mind, a want for him to be the one to say it because I don't think I can—that we are more than just friends.

"Because you're better than that, Shelby!" he says. "You're too good to sleep with some guy just to keep a Promise."

"But you're not too good to fuck Anna Clemens? She's just a social climber. How can you even *like* her?"

Jonas looks taken aback, like I've struck him. He exhales and rises.

"You're sleeping with someone for a Promise. I slept with Anna because I wanted to at the time. The fact that your mom died doesn't mean your reasons are better than mine or you're better than Anna."

He gives me a strange look—part pity, part angry, all cold—then walks toward the door. I hear him pause in the foyer for a moment, then the door open and shut. I crawl across the living room to peer out the blinds, and I watch Lucinda pulling out of my driveway.

I shouldn't have said that. I rise and go to the door, maybe I can catch him, call out, we can talk, we can fix this. But I freeze when I see it on the table in the foyer. Wrinkled and soft-looking, folded up with the title facing me: *Life List*, written across the top in bubble script.

What do I do?

You've gotta be honest with the people you love.

Maybe Dad's right about that—no, not maybe. I know he's right. I know I should have told Jonas the truth, that something has changed, that the idea of him with Anna made me feel sick. I should have told him because I love him, definitely as a friend, maybe as more.

But I'm afraid. Especially now, because I know Jonas was right about one thing at least—I've called girls like Anna whores, judged them, hated them, but I'm not better than them. I'm not better than Jonas. I'm trying to have sex, just like they are. Does that mean I'm a slut?

I don't know.

So what do I do now, Dad? I need advice to go with your advice.

I take the list delicately in my hands and retreat to my bedroom—I put it on my desk and stare at it, like I'm trying to figure out a way to save its life. Trying to find a way to save Jonas and me.

7 days before

Two days after my fight with Jonas, I eat all of the cross-shaped chocolate from the goodie bags. If I can't get laid, I'm going to get fat. I leave a chocolate for Dad on the dining room table; he never mentions it, but I notice it's gone when we're walking out the door for our second and last dance lesson together.

The feeling of dread that washed over me when we arrived at the first dance lesson is conspicuously absent this time around—I guess knowing what's inside Madame Garba's lair makes it a little less terrifying. Dad pays the girl at the front counter, and we make our way to the back of the studio, where once again the little kids are finishing up a Latin dance class. I wonder how Jonas and I would have handled a class like that as children. I wonder how many of these kids will grow up to be friends with their dance partners.

I wonder how many of them will grow up to be more.

And then I hate myself for wondering all of that when Jonas is the last thing I want to think about. *Focus, Shelby,* I think as we file in and begin our waltz class, Madame Garba barking out the count structure. *Don't think about Jonas. Focus on anything. Focus on the waltz, even.*

This time around, Dad and I are able to keep the beat decently, but it seems we're forever destined to stomp on each other's feet. We clumber around, snickering at our equal lack of grace and drawing a few sideways glances from the other dancers who wonder what the laughter is about. It attracts the attention of Madame Garba, who creaks her way over to our side of the studio.

"Elbows up, Sara. Lift through the chest," Garba snaps. It takes me a moment to realize her hawkish eyes are on me and she's merely confused my name.

"It's Shelby," Dad tells her, but Garba flips her hand at him and moves on. He shrugs at me and we continue to spin around the room; I catch flashes of my own eyes in the mirror every few steps. *Sara.* That's the name of the character in *A Little Princess*, Sara Crewe. I smile a little at the mistake and think of Mom reading the story to me.

Madame Garba teaches us some fancy steps that Dad and I are afraid to try more than once—dips and turns that Mona and her father pick up almost immediately. Watching them spin around each other doesn't bother me as much as it did at the last class—yeah, they can do that fancy little arm thing, but...it doesn't matter. After all, Dad and I aren't doing so terribly at the basics anymore. I guess that's enough for me.

The music dies down and everyone stops; Dad and I step away from each other. The room applauds and Madame Garba gives a yellow-toothed smile, then complains loudly to the male assistant that she needs a cigarette break before the next class.

"I guess I'll see you at the ball, Shelby! I'm so excited to see what everyone's dress looks like. It'll be a sea of white," Mona says, giggling as she gathers her purse from the back of the room.

"Not entirely," I say, shrugging. "My dress is blue."

Mona tries her best not to look horrified, but her best isn't quite good enough—I see her eyes flicker from me to her father. To my surprise, he looks more delighted than horrified.

"Blue, Shelby? That sounds lovely!" he says warmly, and gives my dad an approving nod.

"I supposed Shelby's always marched to the beat of her own drummer," Dad says, smiling at me briefly. Mona is also smiling now, but it looks so forced and tense that I think she might burst a blood vessel in her eye. I imagine her as one of those cartoon robots, head spinning and smoking. *Blue! Blue, not white! Shelby is wearing blue! KAPOW! EXPLOSION!* Jonas would get a kick out of that image.

Wait. No. You're mad at Jonas. Don't forget. Don't think about him, I remind myself, though I'm not sure why I'm still mad at him now—is it because he slept with Anna, because he called me out on being a hypocrite, or because he didn't choose me?

Maybe all three.

"Well, that's pretty much it, isn't it?" Dad says as we make our way to the dance-studio parking lot. "We've got the questionnaires, but there's nothing else to make or plan or learn or... anything."

"I guess not," I say, shrugging. As we pull out of the parking lot, I see Madame Garba leaning out the back of the dance studio, smoking a long cigarette. I think about her calling me Sara Crewe instead of Shelby Crewe.

I know this is some sort of blasphemy, being my mother's daughter and all, but I've always liked the movie version of *A Little Princess* better than the book. For one, in the movie you get to see that scene when the Indian guy fills Sara's attic with all sorts of cool decorations and foods and things. But also, I like that in the end, you discover that Sara's father—who everyone thought was dead—has been living right across the street from her. He had amnesia and couldn't remember who she was, but then he sees Sara and it all rushes back to him, and they live happily ever after. In the book version, it isn't her father living across the street; it's her father's old friend. He takes her in and is nice and all, but I always felt like that was sort of a consolation prize.

Mom and I sometimes argued when *A Little Princess* was up in the bedtime story rotation. I wanted her to tell the movie's ending, and she insisted on reading the story as it was written. But there was nothing *magical* about the book ending, if you ask me. One of my favorite parts of the movie is the scene when Sara realizes her father was there all along, right across the street. Living with that awesome Indian guy who could make things float.

That's real magic.

4 days before

Less than a week before the ball, Dad has gone into paperwork-related overdrive and I'm stuck running a million ball-related errands. The decorating committee needs more pink crepe paper, the music needs to be put together on a playlist, the cake needs to be paid for. I still haven't finished my questionnaire—though I think Dad and I have totally given up on finding time to finish those, much less go over them together. I still need to pick out the passage or quote or something to read in front of everyone. I went through *To Kill a Mockingbird*, but I can't figure out what passage Mom used, so I think I'll need to look elsewhere....

One thing at a time, I think, exhaling. Dad is gone, something to do with figuring out the table setup, but he asked me to look at the playlist used at the last Princess Ball, to see if there were any songs I wanted to add. He said it would be "on the table, in plain sight," but given that there seems to be about four thousand different forms, packets, and contracts on this table, it's sort of like looking for a needle in a stack of needles. I carefully shuffle through everything, trying to make sure everything gets put back in whatever stack it belongs in. Nothing resembling a playlist anywhere—I lift a stack of Princess Ball brochures to check under them.

Mom smiles back at me.

I freeze, set the brochures down carefully. It's the picture of her at the Princess Ball, crisp and glossy, I guess because it's been sitting in a box or frame instead of being handled frequently. She's wearing that dress with the sleeves whose puffiness is rivaled only by her hair. My grandfather is on her right, tall and young-looking with tinted glasses, and they're in front of a baby-pink backdrop with white roses in vases around them.

I sit down in Dad's chair slowly, still staring at the photo. It isn't quite how I remembered it—I was so focused on the puffy sleeves that I never saw the way the bodice of the dress is actually really pretty. I didn't remember the roses, and I certainly didn't remember there being a little cross necklace around her neck. Mom wasn't very religious, and religious jewelry definitely wasn't her style...but was it then? Did something change, or did I just never understand my mom's beliefs to begin with?

Maybe it's just a piece of jewelry. Something my grandfather gave her, something she owned that was pretty more than iconic. But still, I can't help but wonder...did Mom think about God the way I do? Did she go to church, wishing she fit in and could say, without a doubt, that God loved her? Did she have questions that couldn't be answered with scripture?

Or do I have those questions only because of losing her?

Maybe even Mom wouldn't get it—why I doubt. Why I question. Maybe no one can understand what this feels like but me. I touch my neck, the spot where the cross charm hangs on Mom's neck. No one can understand because... they really don't know any better than I do. No matter what they think, how sure they are they've got everything figured out, they're as in the dark as I am.

They might know Bible verses and hymns and stories and history, but no one can ever really understand God—no one can ever really know why he took my mom, why he lets bad things happen to good people. And no one can really know what I need from God, or what God needs from me—more prayer, more faith, more devotion...no one really knows.

Dad *might* get it—he'd be the closest to understanding, I think. He knows what it was like to lose her. Is the promise that "Mom's in a better place" enough for him, or does he question, too? I wonder what he'd say if I told him all this, how no one can answer my questions, how I'm not always sure what I believe. Would he side with the Princess Ball committee, the church, Pastor Ryan? Or with me?

I wouldn't ask him to choose sides, though. I don't want him in the middle of me and anyone—it might hurt him, and I don't want to hurt him. Not because of the Promises.

Because I'm his daughter.

I still need the Promises. I still need them to grab onto. But maybe not being able to grab onto God isn't the worst thing after all. Maybe I'm not meant to grab on. Maybe I'm meant to grab on later, or onto a whole different religion, or quietly. Maybe I'll never be able to go to a church and believe like everyone else does, and maybe I'll still be angry sometimes, still feel like things were unfair. Or maybe someday I'll have jewelry with a religious icon on it.

And maybe—no, not maybe, *definitely*—Jonas was right about more than just Anna. She had sex for her own reasons. Mona believes for her own reasons. Mom wore a cross necklace for her own reasons. Even Pastor Ryan is a pastor for his own reasons.

And I doubt. For reasons no one else can understand. And maybe that's okay.

1 day before

The doorbell rings at seven thirty Saturday night. I take a moment to run my fingers through my hair and straighten my shirt before going down. I went all out and bought the bra that matches the panties Ruby got me. If that's not dedication, I don't know what is.

"Shelby? There's a boy here for you," my dad's voice rings up the stairs. I cringe—Dad meeting my one-night stand wasn't exactly in the game plan. There's nothing to be done about it now, though, I guess. I swallow and head to the door.

Dad and Jeffery are talking about the weather, which seems so ridiculously appropriate that I almost laugh. When they hear me on the stairs, they both turn to look at me. I look at Dad first—he's smiling, looks carefree, like he's not the tiniest bit worried about the boy at the door being around his daughter. I feel guilty about my plans for a flash of a moment, a moment filled with images of both Dad's and Jonas's faces.

I have to keep the Promises. I have to do this.

Even as I think it, though, I know this isn't just about the Promises anymore. I want to do this because I'm curious. I want to do this because I dare God to make me feel guilty for it. I have my own reasons for doubting and believing and having sex, and I *want to do this*.

I reach the door. Jeffery is smiling in a way that's so genuine and friendly, I swear he's three seconds from being cast in a Disney Channel movie.

"Have a nice time!" Dad says brightly, and I hold back a cringe.

"Thanks, Dad. See you later tonight," I answer. Jeffery and I step out the door and walk toward his car — it's an old Jeep, dark green and covered in a layer of dust.

"So," Jeffery says as we reach the end of my driveway. "Did Ruby tell you about my shameless crush on you?"

I laugh a little nervously. "She didn't put it that way, exactly, but that's nice to hear."

Jeffery runs ahead to the passenger side to open the door for me. The car's interior is cleaner than the outside and reminds me a little bit of Lucinda — maybe it's the stale french fries smell or the hard, aged feel of all the surfaces.

Jeffery drives slow, stopping completely at all the stop signs and never running a yellow light. It's almost eight by the time we arrive at Harry's for dinner.

"So," Jeffery says as our food arrives, "who is the guy you're always sitting with, if he's not your boyfriend?"

Damn, and I was doing a halfway decent job of not thinking about Jonas. Kinda. Sorta.

Okay, so I haven't been able to get him out of my head.

"Just a friend," I answer quickly. "Sort of. We're fighting at the moment, actually."

Jeffery raises his eyebrows. "Anything serious?"

"Not really. He just kept some secrets from me. Hurt my feelings, that's all."

"Ah. Maybe he had a reason?"

"A bad one," I answer, and Jeffery laughs.

"I hope you guys make up, though. For the Biscuit's sake. You two are, like, half of our business," he says, then eats three french fries at once.

There's nothing wrong with Jeffery; in fact, I can see myself developing a crush on him given enough time. By the time dinner and the movie that follows are over, it's getting late but we still haven't entirely run out of things to talk about. It's trivial stuff, little things — favorite color, which countries you've been to, any siblings — but it's nice in that regard. Nothing complicated, nothing that requires too much emotion or thought. When we pull into his driveway, he stares at me for a moment.

"My mom and stepdad are in Maui," he explains. "I was thinking that you could come in for a while, if you're interested." I nod and climb out of the Jeep before he can run around to open the passenger-side door.

He gives me the tour of the house, introduces me to his Labrador. But we speak in hushed voices, bedroom voices, and it isn't long before he suggests we watch TV on the couch. I draw closer and closer to him as the show goes on until, finally, he inhales and turns toward me. He kisses my cheek softly, tenderly even. I turn and find his lips on mine.

He's a good kisser — maybe the best I've ever kissed. I

lean back on the couch, pulling him down over me. Clothing falls to the floor in piles, the TV irregularly lighting up our bodies. I grab a condom from my purse and, without asking, he rips it open.

He puts the condom on and leans over me, and then everything tightens for a moment, a strange, dizzying feeling that makes me inhale.

I stare at the ceiling and bite my lip as Jeffery begins to move back and forth—it isn't painful, isn't pleasurable, isn't anything, to be honest. It's like shaking hands or waving or something else sterile, almost businesslike. Jeffery's weight is heavy on me, and I wrap my arms around his shoulders, not because I love him, but because it makes it easier to breathe.

I can't believe I'm doing this.

And then I think of the one person I probably shouldn't be thinking about while having sex: Mom.

I think about the Promises, I think about her hands, I think about the headstone with the *love* phrase. I think about the french fries, and how they were cold when she finally got them but she tried to eat them anyway. I think about her in heaven with God, her in heaven without God. About how I realize now that I'll never be able to pinpoint God, to grab onto him and blame him. All I can do is grab onto love—the certainty that wherever Mom is, she still loves me. That Dad still loves me. That I will forever love both of them.

Jeffery is breathing heavy, murmuring something in my ear. There's still no pain, just pressure near my stomach and a gentle, whirling sensation. It makes me feel alive, makes me feel *present* the same way running or swimming or inhaling a summer breeze has a way of making me feel that way. He kisses me, and for a moment, I wonder if this is how Jonas would've kissed me, if I'd ever given him the chance. I immediately know that the answer is no — Jonas is the closest one to me, the one I grab onto when the ground crumbles. He'd kiss me like *that*, not like someone I just met.

He'd kiss me like someone who loves me. And I'd kiss him back the same way. It's so clear, so obvious, that I can't believe I didn't realize it before: I've been in love with Jonas for years.

Promise Two: Love as much as possible.

Jeffery shudders, grips my shoulders tightly, and it's over. He breathes heavily and pulls himself off me, then gives me a kind smile, but my mind is too cluttered to return it.

I forgot about Promise Two. But it was the most important, because no matter what else happens, the love is still there. Love isn't a question of faith, even if God is. I thought it was such an easy Promise, such an obvious one, but this whole time, I never realized what it really meant.

"You okay?" Jeffery asks breathlessly, sliding off the couch beside me.

"I'm fine," I say. Immediately after saying it, I realize it's true.

"You're sure?" he asks.

"Yeah." I get up and hunt for my clothes in the darkness. Silence filters over the room, not awkward but heavy and still. I hurriedly pull on my shirt.

"Um…can I tell you something?" Jeffery says, his voice

a little quiet. I turn to him, surprised by his tone. "My father died. Six months ago."

I sit down beside him, unsure how to respond—how is it that I, of all people, don't know what to say to him? No wonder everyone babbles when I tell them about Mom. Appropriate responses are hard to come by.

Jeffery continues, "Ruby told me that this was about the sex and said it had something to do with your mom dying."

"She what?" I ask.

Jeffery shrugs and sits up, looking sheepish. "After Dad died, I drove all the way to Arizona and back. Didn't sightsee, didn't do touristy stuff, didn't stay in Arizona more than about eight hours. I get it," he says. "Grief kind of takes weird forms sometimes. I just wanted to tell you because I don't think you're weird for . . . you know."

I smile. "Thank you."

"Anytime," Jeffery says. "Though I wasn't making up that crush on you, so I'm a little worried you're going to think I'm a man whore now, sleeping with you on the first date, even if I know it's what you wanted."

I laugh. "No, not at all. You were a real gentleman, honestly."

"So . . . you might be interested in a second date with this gentleman?" he asks.

I look down. Jeffery's face falls. "It's nothing you did," I say. "It's just that . . . I think I'm in love with someone else."

"Wow, you're a real heartbreaker," Jeffery says, but he smiles a little.

"Sorry I...kinda used you for sex," I tell Jeffery glumly.

He shrugs. "I'm not too upset. Hey, it's not a bad way to get used."

＊　＊　＊　＊

I'm in a little bit of a daze by the time I make it home—not because I'm sad, not because I'm confused, but because it's simply...over. All the worrying, all the stressing, the lists, the hype...it's done.

And the act itself wasn't that life-changing—well, the *sex* itself wasn't. Everything else was.

I wave to Jeffery and slip into the house. Luckily, Dad is fast asleep in front of the television. He doesn't stir when I walk in, and as per usual he is surrounded by paperwork. I sneak over and pick up his watery glass from the coffee table and turn the television off. As I reach for the remote, I see the paper he was last studying. The title splayed across the top reads:

FATHER QUESTIONNAIRE

I haven't finished mine—didn't even plan on finishing it, to be honest. But Dad was going over his? Did he finish it? I wonder...I glance between Dad and the paper, then slowly, quietly pull it away from him. I leave the glass in the kitchen and head up to my bedroom. My desk lamp is on, casting the room in pale violet light the color of its shade. I fall into my bed with my clothes on and look at the paper in my hands.

I hesitate. I shouldn't read it without his knowing.

But I unfold his questionnaire anyway, then flatten it across my pillow.

1. Your Name: Doug Crewe
2. Daughter's Name(s): Shelby Crewe
3. Spouse's Name: Jennifer Louise Crewe

Her full name, written in such clear and precise script that it looks a little bit like a child practicing his own signature. There's a thick dot of ink at the end of the final "e" on our last name, like he paused to admire her name for a moment after writing it.

4. How much quality time do you spend with your daughter exclusively on any given day?
Not very much

True enough, until this ball madness started.

5. Do you want to be closer to your daughter?
Yes

I roll my eyes at the question. Who would put "no" for that?

6. What are some things you have in common with your daughter?

I'm not sure—I wish I knew.

7. What is your favorite memory of your daughter?

I inhale before reading Dad's answer, remembering my own response to the question about him. I wonder if he had as hard a time coming up with an answer.

Watching Jenny hold Shelby for the first time.

It wasn't just me who loved her. I read on—there's another line, written in pencil like it was tacked on afterward.

Cake tasting day

I smile.

8. Are you willing to help your daughter live a pure life?
?

A question mark? What was unclear about that question? I mean, I know he isn't likely to flex his computer-programming muscles to keep me from making out with some guy, but surely he's willing to help me in some regard, right?

9. What is the purpose of the Princess Ball, in your opinion?

There are heavy pen marks over one sentence, his crossed-out original answer:

~~To learn how to help my daughter live a pure life.~~

But under that he's written:

I want to get to know Shelby better.

Promise One: Love and listen to my father. This whole time I've been obeying his every word, following all the rules, saying all the right things. But I never did what he really wanted all along.

Because I was never really listening.

The day of

My phone rings at 9:03 the day of the Princess Ball.

"Shelby? I'm coming over, okay?" It's Ruby.

"Huh? Uh, sure. It's early...."

"I have to be at the Biscuit by ten thirty, so it had to be early. Sorry. You can stay in bed—the spare is still under that green flowerpot, right?"

Unfortunately, the fifteen minutes it takes Ruby feels only like a few seconds. Before I know it, Ruby is bursting into my room. She gives me the once-over, then shrugs and sits down on the edge of my bed. I scoot over to give her more room as she twirls her fingers around the loose threads of my comforter.

"Hi," she says after I don't speak.

I nod at her and rub my eyes.

"So...is everything okay?" Ruby asks.

"Yeah, why?"

"I just...well, I talked to Jeffery...and he said you guys did have sex, but then you didn't call me, so I wondered if you regretted it and got pissed at me for suggesting it or..."

"Oh," I say. "No. I don't regret having sex. I was just

thinking about it last night, that's all. And...I kinda think I had it all wrong. Everything."

"Explain," Ruby says, spinning around so she's lying down next to me. She touches her pointer fingers to her chin in a mock psychiatrist way and I smile.

"I forgot," I say. "I forgot about Promise Two because I was so busy finding ways to keep One and Three. And I'm starting to think that I got Promise One wrong—it was love and listen to my father, but I've been treating him like a stranger, just blindly following orders. That's not really loving or listening."

Ruby doesn't say anything, so I go on.

"So that leaves Promise Three...but..." I drift off as my mind swirls. "How am I living without restraint if I'm letting the Promises force me into having sex with someone I don't really care about? The Promises themselves restrain me."

"But doesn't that mean that Promise Three negates the other Promises?" Ruby says.

"Maybe," I say. "I thought obeying them would make me closer to Mom, would bring her back in a weird way. Maybe make me okay with her death. But the truth is, I don't think Mom wanted me to treat her Promises like strict rules. I think she just wanted me to be happy. And Dad to be happy. And both of us to remember her and love her and find love in everyone else."

"You sound heartbeats away from writing a truly brilliant pop song," Ruby says with a grin. "If only 'All You Need Is Love' wasn't taken."

"Damn the Beatles."

"So are you glad you did it, then?" Ruby finally asks.

"I think I had to. I had to do it to start to understand everything else. And I'm not sure I totally do yet.... It's like all these tiny pieces of my life are beginning to make sense."

Ruby nods. "When you sort it all out, let me know. I'd love for it all to make sense by the time I have sex."

I widen my eyes and look at her. "By the time?"

Ruby shrugs. "I'm still a virgin."

"What?" For a moment, I'm almost angry, but it fades to surprise quickly. "But you knew all that stuff! You gave me the panties!"

Ruby blushes — something I've rarely seen her do. "I'm not saying I'm an innocent schoolgirl, Shel, but knowledge isn't the same thing as experience. I guess I do sort of act the part, though. I should've told you. I'm sorry I suck so bad. But think about it, isn't it going to be hilariously weird, me coming to you for sex tips in the future?"

We laugh together, then lie in silence for a second.

"So, to totally jump subjects in the least disrespectful way possible," Ruby says, "want to see my photos? I finished them."

"Which ones?" I ask.

"From the park. A few weeks ago?"

"Oh yeah!" From before the LOVIN plan, from before I had sex and planned a ball. It feels like ages ago. She leans over me and pulls her purse up. Inside is a piece of cardboard from a Flying Biscuit to-go box. It's folded in half and held shut by a scrap of ribbon, protecting a thick stack of photos. Ruby unties the ribbon and the photos spill out onto my bedspread like fallen leaves.

I'm only a silhouette, the sun brilliant behind me and scattered tree limbs. My hair flies out behind me as I fall through the air — you can't see the fountain — into the arms of a waiting boy. Jonas, reaching toward me.

"So, I heard you and Jonas got in a fight," Ruby says.

I sigh. "Yeah. He slept with Anna Clemens."

"And that's a problem?"

"Yes."

"Why?" She asks the question like she knows the answer, a sly grin on her face.

I bite my lip, unsure if I want to say it aloud. It'll change everything. But I take a deep breath and speak anyway. "It's a problem because I... have feelings for him. I just didn't realize it."

"What about the fact that Jonas 'has feelings' for *you*?" she says, using quote-hands and rolling her eyes.

Hearing Ruby say that makes me feel very girly and fluttery and *happy*.

"See how good I am at this puppet master thing? I totally called this years ago," Ruby teases. "Call him, Shelby. Call him and make up and be best friends and then go kiss and let it be awkward and great."

I flush. "You're assuming he's going to not be mad that I slept with Jeffery. Not to mention, last time we spoke, we were fighting."

"He slept with Anna. You both had to get some action elsewhere to realize how much you wanted each other. And it was just a fight. It happens. So anyway, back to my plan—call him, be best friends, awkward kissing. You know how much I love awkward kissing, Shelby. Have you *seen* my collection of quirky romantic comedies?"

I sigh and shake my head. "I will, I will, I just...this ball, and then last night with Jeffery and...I need to finish things with the Princess Ball before I can tell him. It's tonight and I don't even have all my stuff together—damn, I'm supposed to find something to read...." I remember, frowning.

"Ugh. Fine. Awkward kissing postponed," she says, making a face. She reaches down again and pulls up a beaten Macy's bag. Inside I see bits and pieces of Ocean Fiesta. "So this dress...there's not a lot a girl can do with a Hello Kitty sewing machine and a million yards of chiffon, but it's *wearable*."

"Thanks, Ruby," I say graciously, sitting up. "Want me to try it on?"

"Nope, 'cause if it doesn't fit I'll feel terrible. And I won't be able to fix it anyway, 'cause that thing took, like, twelve hours to finish."

"But...if it doesn't fit, what will I wear to the ball?"

"I'm pretty sure only Cinderella is authorized to say things like that. But it doesn't matter—it'll fit. I kind of just want you to be surprised, to be honest. Oh, and I put some extra makeup in that bag—you need to wear more blush and some sparkly powder. Sparkly powder was made for balls, even creepy virgin ones."

"Right," I say, nodding. "I owe you big."

"Yep. You're gonna need to order copious amounts of food next time you swing by the Biscuit. And maybe tip thirty, forty percent," she grins. I can feel hints of tears welling up—I'm happy about the dress, somehow excited about working the whole love thing out. Ruby looks perplexed for a minute, then leans forward to hug me.

"Christ, Shelby. You get laid and suddenly you're all emotional," she teases.

"No, it's not like that," I say. "I think I'm just... I'm just ready to go and get it over with. Which is almost exactly what I said about getting laid, oddly enough."

Ruby grins as she rises to leave, then calls back over her shoulder. "Just remember this, Shel—you got laid. But that doesn't mean you won't ever make love."

The ball

A few hours later I throw on what little makeup I have. It isn't much, but Ruby's blush does seem to light up my cheeks, and the sparkly powder makes my skin look smoother than it really is. I straighten my hair, then wrap a towel around myself and dash back to the bedroom for the gown.

It spills from the bag with far less fabric than before. When I hold it up, I realize that half the poofiness is gone. Ruby cut off the spaghetti straps and sliced away a few layers of crinoline. There's slick blue satin across the bodice, and some sort of old-fashioned lace and beadwork around the neck.

I'm not so sure about this. I drop the towel and step into the dress nervously. It'll fit, she promised. And besides, there's no going back now unless I wear that lime-sherbet monstrosity from the winter formal. I slip my hands into the new straps, which are gathered satin and sit on the edge of my shoulders. I feel like they should slide off, but they stay put as I open my closet door to see myself in the mirror on the other side.

I inhale.

It's beautiful. There's not another way to put it, really. The frothy Ocean Fiesta now looks part ball gown, part sari. Tiny pearlescent beads flicker inside the lace, and the satin that slants down the front of the skirt gives way to only a few layers of flattened, graceful chiffon that moves like water around me when I spin to the side.

Ruby was right. I *do* owe her.

I grab a book, then frantically flip through it—I think I've finally figured out a passage to read aloud. I can't believe I didn't think of it sooner, really. It's short, and I'm not sure it'll make sense to the rest of the Princess Ball goers but... I'm also not sure I care about that. I find a pen and scribble down the lines, shut the book, and walk down the hallway to the staircase. The dress fabric rustles behind me.

Dad is downstairs watching television, slouched so that I'm sure his dress shirt will be wrinkled when he stands up. He turns around as he hears me hit the bottom step.

"Shelby," he says, raising his eyebrows. "That dress is beautiful."

"Thanks," I say, resisting the urge to twirl around in circles and make the skirt flow out. "Ruby...fixed it."

"I was about to say," Dad says, nodding. "That isn't exactly Kaycee's style."

We stare at each other.

"Well...ready to do this?" Dad says, his voice a little worried.

"We've come this far," I say. He grabs his coat and holds open the front door, and we're off.

It doesn't look like a church gym. The sidewalk is lined in Christmas lights and there's a banner hung over the gym sign that reads *31st Annual Princess Ball* in swirly writing. Two men are standing at the door in tuxedos, welcoming people inside.

"Doug!" one of them calls out. Dad waves. "I've got to tell you," the guy says as we draw closer. "You've done an amazing job. The place looks beautiful."

"Ah, well, the decorating committee did that," Dad says.

"With the decorations you ordered! You know how to get the job done, Doug, that's for sure," the other man says. "And little Shelby Crewe! You look lovely." I force a smile as they wave us inside.

The ceiling lights in the gym are turned off; instead the room has a pinkish hue on account of dozens of tall floor lamps, candles on every table, and a spotlight that illuminates a stage built in the back. A long table decked out in pink tablecloths stretches down one wall, and the floor is covered in silver heart-shaped confetti. On the opposite side is a long table of goodie bags, baskets full of white roses, and the elegant white envelopes that contain the vows the fathers and daughters will recite later.

Pastor Ryan watches from a table near the front, a quiet, mousy woman I assume is his wife sitting beside him. Gentle piano music drifts out over the speakers and mingles with the sound of girls giggling, laughing, dancing with one another while their fathers watch proudly.

"We're sitting there," Dad says, pointing to the table with the pastor. "The whole planning committee is."

I take my seat while Dad does a lot of handshaking. The table is covered in champagne glasses that are full of sparkling white grape juice, according to the bottle near the middle of the table. White rose petals are strewn about, and a little paper centerpiece with the *31st Annual Princess Ball* logo rests in the center.

"We're about to start the readings, right before dinner is served. Did you have a hard time choosing your passage, Shelby?" Pastor Ryan asks.

"I did," I confess, "but I finally chose one."

"Excellent — oh, wow, looks like it's time to get started," Pastor Ryan interrupts himself. Dad sits down beside me as Pastor Ryan makes his way to the stage. I take a long sip of my grape juice. I can't believe this is finally happening.

"Ladies and gentlemen," Pastor Ryan says from the stage. He's talking into a microphone attached to a podium surrounded by so many white roses that I fully expect to see them on some sort of endangered plants list tomorrow. The chatter of the ballroom dies down. "Welcome to our thirty-first annual Princess Ball!"

There's an explosion of cheering, and I think I hear Mona's voice above the rest. It settles down as Pastor Ryan holds up his hands.

"I'm excited, too! Fathers, daughters, you'll all be so proud, so happy that you came here tonight. That you're taking a vow, making a commitment to each other that will last long after you've grown out of those dresses, ladies.

"But before we get this under way, I'd like for the daughters to come up here..." he waits until we stand, "...come up here and form a line. Fathers, each daughter has found a line from a poem, a book perhaps, a play, something that she feels represents your relationship, or the importance of the relationship between fathers and daughters in general."

I try to get near the back of the line, but girls keep moving and readjusting to stand near their friends. To my dismay, Mona bounds up to stand by me. She's wearing her mother's pearls and a bright grin.

The first girl steps up to the microphone—she's vaguely familiar from school. She's clutching a slip of paper, which she unfolds, hands shaking a little. What is she nervous about? About messing up? Embarrassing herself? Embarrassing her father?

I look out into the audience, wondering if I'll be able to pick her father out from the sea of men. I'm surprised by how easy it is, especially once she begins to read—a quote by Sigmund Freud. Her dad is the one beaming, the one watching her like he's never been so proud, all over a tiny little line. It makes me smile.

The line shifts forward as the next girl steps up. It's easy to pick out her father, too, easy to see who it is who loves her. I wonder if she knows what I can see from here, that he'll love her if she messes up or falls down the stage or whatever.

That all the fathers here love their daughters like that. Mine included.

Mona next. She shimmies up her dress before stepping into the lights and pulling out a card. Hers is the longest reading yet, a passage from Shakespeare about the importance of honoring one's father, filled with lots of dramatic pauses. She gives a little curtsy before stepping offstage.

Honor your father—it sounds so archaic, but I guess it's pretty much the same as Promise One: *Love and listen to my father.* I glance at the audience, looking for Dad. He's smiling at me.

He'll love me no matter what happens. No matter what I vow. I kept the Promises for Mom, yet here I am, planning to fake a Promise to Dad? Planning to lie to him, when the truth is, he's going to love me no matter what I decide about my own purity? It's the first time I've thought of a loophole as a lie, but really . . . that's all it is.

"Shelby, it's your turn," someone hisses behind me.

"Huh? Oh!" I step up to the podium slowly, squinting in the light. I can't see anyone in the ballroom. It reminds me of how people with near-death experiences describe looking at heaven, only there's nothing warm and peaceful about this light. I unfold the scrap of paper with my passage on it, crumpled from being death-gripped.

Just read it. Hurry, read it and get off the stage.

But even though my lines are right in front of me, all I can think of is what Dad told me. *You've gotta be honest with the people you love.*

Someone coughs nervously, and I realize I've been staring at the light for too long.

"All...um...all girls..." I stop. There's something I want to say more than this.

"I'm...um...I'm supposed to read this passage from a book." There are a few scattered, confused claps from within the light, but I shake my head and they fall silent.

"But my dad said something about being honest the other day, and I think that's what I want to say instead of this. I want to be honest about...um...what I learned during this whole Princess Ball...thing."

People shift uncomfortably, me included.

"And that's that...vowing to be close to your father isn't enough. You have to actually do it, because a promise has power only when you *decide* to keep it. Being close to your father or living without restraint or promising to be pure, it's all your decision. And maybe you'll decide to live a pure life or maybe you won't, maybe it'll be something in between—but you've gotta be honest with the people you love. Making fake promises while wearing a fancy dress...that isn't enough. Promises take more work than that."

I breathe deeply.

I fold up my paper.

And I step down from the podium.

If this were a movie, there'd be thunderous applause right about now—I mean, that was a semi-kick-ass speech if you ask me. Instead, everyone stares. Some of the girls lean toward their fathers nervously as I walk past, like they might catch my crazy. Mona half giggles in her fluffy marsh-mallowlike dress.

And then I see Dad.

He's still sitting at the front table with the rest of the committee. I can't see him clearly first, my eyes still adjusting to the change from bright stage lights to the dim ballroom. As he comes into view, I scramble to interpret the expression on his face. Yeah, he'll love me no matter what I do, but that doesn't mean I could blame him for being angry, or embarrassed, or some lethal combination of the two—after all, I just negated some of the Princess Ball's validity, the purpose of everyone sitting at our table, of making the vows, his purpose as coordinator....I can't sit down at that table right now—I have to get out of here. Dad rises as I pass him and follows me out the door as another girl gets up to read her carefully prepared passage.

*   *   *   *

It's oddly silent out here in the hallway, and the rustling of my dress sounds like little explosions as we make our way down the short hallway and into the church classroom with the Picture Book Jesus paintings. Dad waits for me to speak, and when I don't, he inhales deeply.

"That was an *interesting* speech, Shelby."

"I know," I answer. "Don't be mad. It's not that I don't think the Princess Ball matters—it does, I just...I feel like there's more to it, and not everyone understands that, so I had to say something. . . ."

"I'm not mad," Dad says slowly. He pauses a long time, like he's choosing his words carefully. "In that questionnaire, the one it seems we forgot to go over, I said that some of my favorite memories and experiences with you were planning this ball. Because there wasn't much before that. Not really."

"Actually, I sort of read your questionnaire," I admit, lowering my chin. Tonight's menu is guilt, guilt, and more guilt.

"Oh," Dad says, though he doesn't seem upset—in fact, he seems sort of surprised. "Was there anything in there . . . I mean . . . well, was it okay?"

"There was one thing," I say. "There was this one question about you helping me live a pure life. You put a question mark. I don't get it."

Dad clears his throat. "Are you worried I put a question mark when what I really meant was no?"

"Not exactly. I mean, maybe—"

"Because that wasn't the debate—whether or not I would help you. The reason I put the question mark was that I didn't know if you'd want my help. I'd . . ." Dad turns a little pink around the edges. "I'd help you with whatever you wanted, Shelby. But it has to be something you want. I always assumed you'd just tell me one day what you needed me for. Actually . . ." Dad shuffles his feet for a moment. "I blame your mom."

211

"For what?"

"Right before your mom died, she made me make these three promises. I thought she was just talking out of her head—she was on so many medicines—but I agreed to them anyway."

All the air seems to have left the room. My eyes widen.

"The first one was to listen when you came to me with something," Dad says. "So I guess I just figured you'd come to me outright. That I wouldn't have to go to you."

I smile. "What was the second?"

"The second was to love as much as possible. Which is easier said than done, sometimes," Dad says thoughtfully. "Anyway, Shelby—I'm not mad. You tried to talk me out of the ball early on. I should have realized you just didn't want to do it, instead of believing all that business about it being finals week and you not liking formal dresses."

I hesitate. "What was the third promise?" I ask, wondering if Dad was supposed to be living a life without restraint, too.

Dad blushes a little. "To get rid of the shirt I was wearing at the time. She said it made me look like a decaying tomato."

We laugh brightly, without worrying about being heard. When we finally compose ourselves a few moments later, we're grinning.

"By the way," Dad says, "what *were* you going to read?"

I look down at the piece of paper that's still in my hand, now wet from my sweaty palms. I hold it out to him. It's from *A Little Princess*. What can I say—if nothing else, it was thematically appropriate? It's from the part of the movie where Sara Crewe stands up to the antagonist, a part I find impossible to not read in Mom's voice.

I am a princess. All girls are. Even if they live in tiny old attics. Even if they dress in rags, even if they aren't pretty, or smart, or young. They're still princesses. All of us. Didn't your father ever tell you that?

Dad reads the line, then nods. "I remember this. I remember your mom reading it to you." I don't answer, because I'm not sure what to say. Dad looks at the words affectionately for a moment, then continues. "I never really told you that, though, did I?"

"That I'm a princess?"

"Yes."

I almost lie to spare his feelings, but after that big speech about being honest, I can't bring myself to do it. "Maybe not in words, exactly, but...I get it. Now, anyway."

"I should have said it specifically, though," Dad says. "I'm sorry."

I smile. "The narrator is eleven, I think. And she's a little damaged. And my need to be called a princess in the literal sense has totally been fulfilled by this ball. Which, by the way—how about I'll forgive you if we don't have to go back in there?"

"You don't want to finish the ball?"

"Not really."

Dad sighs. "Me neither. Maybe it was planning it, but I'm over the whole thing. And I've been dreading that waltz all week. But there is one thing we have to go back in for. It was supposed to be a surprise, but…"

"What is it?"

"I thought you'd like it. It's in the ballroom, though. I don't know if we'll be able to see it now."

"Are you kidding? We can sneak in!" I say, delighted. Dad, pulling some sort of Princess Ball prank. I have to know.

"Sneak in? It's just by the door—"

"Even better."

We make our way back to the ballroom. They've just starting eating, and the room is buzzing with caterers rushing around tables with semiwilted salads. It provides an excellent cover for slipping back inside. We duck down near a drink cart, out of the planning committee's view.

Dad lifts a finger and points. I follow his direction to the cake. Perfect, tall, delicately iced. Staring at me from the side of the cake, drawn at the very bottom in thin icing, is R2D2, dancing with Princess Leia.

My mom was taken from me. But then, six years later, I ended up with a father I didn't have before.

3 hours after

Despite the fact that we are no longer actually participating in the Princess Ball, Dad insists on staying to help clean up. We watch the rest of the ball from the closed-circuit television, eating snacks stolen from the church kitchen. The waltz is the best part—the sparkly white dresses of almost a hundred girls poof out as they whirl around in their fathers' arms. Dad and I imagine them doing "Thriller" instead and laugh together, though I am kind of mad I spent two days learning to waltz only to miss the damn thing. By the time we get home, it's just after midnight.

Lucinda is parked at the end of our driveway. I look to the door and see Jonas leaning against it, a tired expression on his face.

For the first time, my heart gets that fluttery feeling you read about in books, and I smile a little.

When Jonas realizes it's our car pulling up, he rises. His eyes meet mine through the windshield, a long, silent conversation. He twirls a single yellow rose between his fingers.

"Jonas!" Dad says, waving as we step out of the car.

"Good to see you again." He walks forward and grabs Jonas's hand in a firm shake.

"You, too, Mr. Crewe." Jonas's eyes dart from Dad back to me. Dad turns to look at me, and I give a small smile. It gets the message across.

"Well, then, I'm gonna go inside....I think *Deadliest Catch* is on again. Marathon, you know," Dad says, jamming his key in the front door, then hurrying through it. I hear the TV turn on and the volume goes way up, louder than normal.

"Hey," Jonas says in a fake casual voice. "I...this is dumb, but you didn't call me after the thing with Jeffery, and then I heard from Ruby you'd gone through with it, and I just...are you okay?"

I smile. "I'm fine. Really."

"So...okay...was it...how was..."

"It was nothing, really," I say. "I thought about Mom, actually. And, well...you."

"Oh."

"Yeah..." I inhale. Silence filters around us.

"I also kind of came to apologize for the stuff I said," Jonas says. "I don't know what I was talking about. I just was irritated and stuff, the whole LOVIN thing...."

"You didn't mean any of it?" I ask, leaning against the front door.

Jonas looks at the rose in his hand. "I didn't mean to yell," he says. "And I should have told you about Anna—"

"I didn't mean to have sex with Jeffery," I interrupt. "I mean, I did, but..."

216

Jonas nods, looking relieved. I relax, so does he. "So," he continues after a deep breath, "you look like a lovely virgin princess. How were the vows?"

"Didn't go through with them. Actually, I delivered a kick-ass speech and walked out."

"How'd your dad take that?"

"Well," I say, smiling.

We stand in silence for a moment, a nervousness I've never experienced before around Jonas. There's so much I want to say, and so much I'm afraid to say.

"So...is that flower for me, in honor of my recent ball attendance?" I nod toward the rose in his hand.

"Um...no, actually," he says, and a grin spreads across his face.

"Oh?"

Jonas meets my eyes, face a little sheepish. "It's for your mom. You know, so you can officially cross it off your list."

I pause, nod slowly. "Hang on just a second." Before Jonas can answer, I dash inside the house and up to my bedroom. The list is there, in my jewelry box. I could keep it. I could do it alone—I've *done* it alone. But why would I want to?

Jonas gives me a curious look when I step back out onto the porch. I hold the list out gingerly. Jonas looks down, smiles a little, takes it from my fingers, and pulls his wallet from his back pocket. He puts the list back in the billfold, in the same spot it's always been, then looks back up at me.

I want to say something—I mean to say something, but I can't find the words. I don't need them, though. Jonas extends a hand, and I fold my fingers into his. We walk to the car, my dress rustling along through the grass, and for a tiny, glimmering, beautiful moment, I forget about purity, I forget about promises, and I forget about faith.

All I can think about is love.